Disappearing Act

by the Author

Nude Untitled, 2001

Beatrice Colin

DISAPPEARING ACT

The Toby Press

First Edition 2002

The Toby Press LLC
www.tobypress.com

ISBN 1 902881 40 0, *hardcover*
ISBN 1 902881 41 9, *paperback*

A CIP catalogue record for this title
is available from the British Library

Designed by Breton Jones, London

Photography by Robert Wheeler

Typeset in Garamond by Jerusalem Typesetting

Printed and bound in the United States by
Thomson-Shore Inc., Michigan

For Theo, Frances and Ewan

I was the shadow of the waxwing slain
By the false azure in the window pane;
I was the smudge of ashen fluff and I
Lived on, flew on, in the reflected sky.

Vladimir Nabokov
from "Pale Fire"

Contents

Act I   page 9

Act II   page 75

Act III   page 155

T he name on the package is Miss Wing Ringling. It is my name. Ringaling for short, Sting Ring by childish acquaintances and Miss Jin Plum by my admirers. I live on the top floor of a tower block opposite another and once walked the tightrope between them. For that I was fined £30 by the council. I never liked floors. Ceilings, ladders, platforms, balconies are fine. But floors are dull, grounded, sort of earthily earthy. That's why I asked for floor 36. It was the least floorish they had.

I was a child circus star, born in a caravan somewhere between Troon and Dunoon. I could swing before I could walk; fly before I could say my own name and was an experienced trapezist and horse acrobat by the time I was six.

Gallop, gallop, hup, tumble tumble, thud, round of applause, thank you.

As I grew, I graduated from spitting sawdust to sweating glitter. Higher and higher, faster and faster and quicker and quicker I jumped as the cheers boomed until they surrounded me like a huge soft cushion. And then I sparkled like a galaxy as I flew shooting-star-style through the spotlight into the dark, darkness of the night sky.

I lied about the tightrope. It's true about the tower block and although I've dreamed about it, I could never do it, not since I lost the use of my legs in the accident. The pony was heavy, as ponies are, and it was an awful long time before they managed to lift him off. As I lay on the ground quite crushed by his weight, I thought that I was outside and the stars on the tent ceiling were real and that the pony was in fact a silver unicorn. Your mind plays funny tricks on you like that sometimes, something to do with natural highs. Shame I had to come down.

They shot the pony. His name was Billy and I had just done a Double-Spin Back-Flip Special on his beautiful broad brown and white back. After all our weeks of practicing, all those sighs and gasps and hearts banging like drums playing the same tune, the silence made me cry.

It was my legs' fault. They became tangled up. Too long, you see. I had just turned 15 and that afternoon I had shaved them for the first time. The doctors told me they would heal and they gave me a pair of calipers but they were a funny shade of American tan so I threw them out of the hospital window and they were stolen by tramps. But I knew the doctors were wrong. Somehow they didn't get better. Somehow I couldn't trust them to carry me along the ground. It was as if they didn't fit me anymore.

I could have kept on going; I had my arms still and the muscles. But everyone at the circus thought I should wait until I got better. They didn't say it but I sensed that they didn't want to turn into a freak show, have a bearded lady and a couple of dwarfs. And besides, nobody can bottom-walk along a tightrope. No one. I've tried.

I don't know why I'm telling you this, Mr 36th floor in the opposite block. It's not as though you can hear and react on cue like the audience does on sitcoms in spurts of the shortest laughter I've ever heard or exclamations of astonishment, which never get past an Aaa.

Well, that's the pip, squeak and hop of it all, I suppose. I knew I would be found eventually.

The package is grubby and has been re-addressed many times. I remember the noise it made this morning, the way it thumped the carpet in a promising kind of way as I lay in bed just waiting to hear the special sound of the post. I receive a lot of mail every day. I answer advertisements in newspaper lonely-hearts columns and send them a photo and write them a letter. They always reply. I am a beautiful nineteen-year-old with the face of an angel, so they say, and the kind of chinked blue eyes that catch the light and look as if they have electric bulbs inside. I arrange dates in expensive restaurants or for the opera. Of course I stand them up. They would only be shocked and that would be embarrassing.

I rip off the brown tape, pick out the staples and pull out a covering letter. It is from a lawyer representing my mother. I ought to explain that I never knew my mother. She joined my circus when she was already pregnant, had me and then promptly died. I was brought up by the Great Barrissimo and his wife Elsie, who took the tickets. They're still on the road. Thurso this week, I think. They told me my mother's name was Helena Heliotrope. She did tricks with mirrors.

Inside the package is a manuscript with two ancient brown coffee rings on the fly page. The lawyer writes that he has spent many months tracking me down through the social services and wishes to inform me that his client, my mother, had instructed him to contact me and pass on my inheritance when I reached eighteen. I shake the padded envelope in case there is anything else hidden inside its velvety brown depths. But there is only the badly typed stack of paper all fastened together with a bulldog clip.

It's hard to explain how I feel. I suppose I am a little disappointed. Diamonds would have been nice. A house by the sea even better. Since I had barely met her, I have no feelings whatsoever about my mother. I am not a sentimental girl, not the type to gaze for hours at old family photographs—if there were any—to see if they held some sort of clue.

I read my admirers' letters before I go anywhere near the manuscript. I look at passport booth snaps of Julius, Rueben, Louis and George and stick them beside the rest in my scrapbook. And only then, after I have skimmed through the letters which are of the usual humdrum variety along the lines of this-is-the-first-time-I've-answered-an-ad and do you like walking, laughing, eating, breathing, nonsense, I turn the first page.

> *Dear Daughter,*
>
> *You are reading this because I am dead. Please don't grieve as I am told that it will be as painless as someone switching off the lights.*
>
> *I know, Little Wing, that I haven't been around much as I would have wished. In fact I have been a useless mother to you. In retrospect it was a bit unfair to bring you so hastily into a world that I am so soon to vacate. And so, after much thought I have decided that the only thing of value I can give you is an account of the strange circumstances of how you came about. You will be shocked, perhaps, but I think you should know. I apologize in advance for the poor quality of this typescript. Having just picked up the skill from a second-hand How To manual, my ability is not honed. Anyway, I hope that my story will be of some use: if not an answer, at least as an explanation.*
>
> *Love,*
>
> *your Mother*

I sigh in a tone that Elsie who took the tickets would have disapproved of because my mother sounds, I decide, like an idiot. And so I throw the whole lot into the dustbin and replace the lid with a bang. Ciao. Bye bye.

Right now, at this very minute, here in my tower block, my body still feels airborne. I dive through air on a set of rings I had fixed up, across the carpet swirls and above the ancient green velvet sofa. My name is Little Wing. I will never touch the ground. Never.

You might see me from the pavement, if you look up. A golden glimpse at a window, a shard of sun which strikes you in the shadows as you stagger along the chipped concrete walkways with your bags of shopping which stretch and rip until they expose your bright tins and your biscuits wrapped like children's treasure. I've watched you down there. I've seen you in your moth-chewed old fur coat and Russian hat as you stumble past the burnt-out litter bin and the rusty traffic sign, you know, the red one with a line through it on which some one has scrawled *I luv Marky* in long spindly letters which dribble. Down in the litter-blustered street, everything looks so crumpled and dead, so hard and scraped, like the very bottom of everything. I know I could never go there. And you, you never look anywhere but one step ahead. Once I shouted.

HEEEEEEeeyyyyyYYYY.

You thought my voice was the wind, pulled your collar up tighter still and shivered. I didn't mean to make you cold.

It is November now.

The Chinese lady who grew vegetables on her balcony doesn't come out anymore. I used to watch her every day setting up her garden in a series of boxes of different heights. Such as a small space. Such a lot of growing things. Now her row of boxes filled with green leaves have turned brown or gone to seed. I wonder if she's died or just lost interest.

Behind your block the city stretches out and its angles look almost soft, like an oriental watercolour with the blue curves and hatch of the gasometer, the charcoal lines of burnt-out buildings, the black river, the purple hills and the pale orange blur of street lights which someone has forgotten to turn off even though it's day. When I first came here I used to spend hours at the window. I couldn't get used to all the people in your block, their lights and noises and taste in curtains. I'd watch them move around their rooms like dolls or sit quite still in front of their television sets or stand in their kitchens waiting for kettles to boil. And then one by one they'd pull down their blinds until they'd all become a part of one great slab of different coloured squares. You have no curtains. Why do you sit so still in the dark?

The telephone rings, prill prill, prill prill and I know that it could only be Julie, my social worker. I let it squeal on and on until I can't stand it, just to disturb her. She knows that the only place I could have gone is straight out of the window. Then I pick it up and say YES and she arranges a time to come up with my shopping even though she isn't supposed to, officially, and do I like pasta sauce in a jar NO, and do I want something from the deli even though it's so expensive and are tinned smoked oysters really good for one everyday and is 2 P.M. tomorrow okay for a little chat and a game of cards where I always cheat and Julie knows but doesn't say.

Julie smiles down the line. She is old, at least forty, but still she wears denim and clogs and coloured tights that match her spectacle frames. She looks like a witch who shops in discount fashion stores. I'm her most difficult case. I am an orphan. I am an invalid. I am a hermit.

But Julie has plans, a place called The Happy House, which will be anything but. I can guess how it will be: I can taste the tea made in germ-infested pots with the sugar in already; I can smell the cooked food kept hot; I can imagine the sight of other people's sadness and hear the sound of fading footsteps on newly disinfected lino. The word they use is sheltered. Doesn't she know that I like the rattle of rain and the moan of the wind on my balcony, when the whole block starts to sway as if it's held up by ropes and pegs, where I can rock back and forth in a cradle of concrete and glass and feel like I belong.

I will not go. She'll make me. I will not go. The council will throw me out on to the suffocating streets. Next Thursday, she says, her voice all tinny and squashed. Your place is booked. And then she tells me and I know she's known for weeks.

"You see, Your Tower Block Is Condemned," she says, just like that, in capital letters.

"It is to be demolished, dismantled, flattened. You have no choice."

For once, I run out of words.

Julie thinks she knows best, thinks she knows me now after three years, thinks she is a good person with the right solutions for wronged people. That makes me laugh.

I notice suddenly that the windows need washing. Strange to think that one day my view (and yours) will be left only to the birds and the occasional plane. I'm staying. I have to. Even if it means I have to be carried out in a box, as Elsie who took the tickets was fond of saying.

You understand. I've seen your face. What will you do now?

I make myself lunch when the siren from the shipyards goes off. It is one o'clock exactly. No one works there anymore but the siren still sounds three times a day. Maybe they have lost its instructions and don't know how to switch it off. Maybe I'm the only one who hears it. I eat one slice of Mothers Pride bread, half a tin of anchovies, one bar of chocolate (with 15% extra) and drink one cup of tea. My supplies are delivered to my door in a crisp box, for a weekly fee of 75p, by that Asian grocer who has the shop on the ground floor next to the bookmaker. I order an orange sometimes just because I like the colour. I have one day and one hour before Julie arrives.

My mother's manuscript is greasy when I pull it out of the dustbin. A few pages have become quite transparent and smell a little fishy. I wrench off the bulldog clip and look at the first page. The text is typed on the thinnest white paper. It is so fine I am tempted to glue it to a hoop and dive right through it. But I don't. First I close my eyes and imagine I am back up on the platform again, back up high in the pinch of the tent where the cobwebs are heavy with tiny jewels of moisture, the air is filled with drifts of dust like fine, fine snow and the wire sings. I breathe in quick and feel the cold air fill me up inside with shivers and blue glow.

And then I start to read.

Act 1

Chapter one

The Genesis of Everything

I will start at the beginning, for beginnings are naturally where stories start. Although where exactly to begin is debatable, I will start with the bare facts and try not, as is my habit, to wander off the point.

My name, in case nobody has told you, is Helena. I am five foot four, my hair is fair, my eyes are a very ordinary blue and I have no distinguishing marks that I am aware of.

A photograph always seems too rigid, as I have the kind of face that changes like wood exposed to the elements, sometimes it suits me, and sometimes it doesn't. So I haven't enclosed one. I'd prefer you to shut your eyes and imagine rather than to examine one frame, one millisecond when I was probably thinking about how to smile successfully.

You may have inherited a few of my traits. I'm sure your skin burns in the sun. Do you find it impossible to spell? Do you hate avocado? Do you read anything and everything from Tolstoy to the backs of cereal packets? It seems strange to me that now I'll never know. When you grew bigger and bigger inside me even when you were supposed to be too little, just a smudge or a tadpole, I could feel you kick and punch and dive just like an acrobat. It was quite peculiar to feel your tiny, quite independent, energy.

And now I watch you in the bottom drawer that I made into a makeshift cot and see your mind spinning with colours and sounds and things with no names. You are such a little thing. I love you dearly. Dearly.

Anyway, I must not waver. I must begin my story. In fact, stories are where everything starts.

I suppose I was always the type of child who needed to read. I devoured miles and miles of pages, pages inhabited by problematic stepmothers and children who saved people from rampant forest fires and animals with remarkable powers and islands which could just float away if they wanted to. Now I think I maybe read too much. Because fiction didn't prepare me well for life but gave me false expectations. I sought out conflict, a certain amount of danger and thirsted for exposition in the most ordinary situations. A satisfactory resolution was, in my belief, my right. Surely, I used to think, my life would all make glorious sense in the end?

But now I'm not too sure. I did have my golden era, my clutch of years where everything seemed gilded with raw excitement and hilarious novelty, where I could be moved by the sight of a half-eaten plate of cornflakes or a crushed train ticket. But as for a plot with three acts and a happy ending, it just didn't happen. At least not in that particular order.

I still wear sequined knickers underneath my old towelling dressing gown. They're a little scratchy on the skin but I like the fact that no one knows they're there but me. The sparkles have their own secret orbit, their place in a little galaxy of nylon knicker fabric. Sometimes I notice single metallic discs shed onto the floor. In the darkness of the room in which I write, it is as if I am raining light.

To start at the very beginning, right at my first gasp of the cold Scottish air, I was born prematurely one raw October morning. My mother had not expected me for at least another two months and was quite put out by the added inconvenience. I was probably just as cross to have arrived a little early and while I am told I had as much black hair on my head as an ape, my tiny pink body was practically transparent. Everybody thought that my visibly beating heart would stop at any moment but after months spent wrapped up in boiled wool blankets lined with cotton wool, my skin turned opaque, I developed a vast appetite for milk and I started to take in the outside world through careful, slatted eyes.

I can't remember much of my first home other than the smell of other people's cooking and the bosom of a very large but now nameless relative. But I do remember that we left in a hurry, checked into a hotel in the middle of the night and the whole episode was never mentioned again.

When I was about seven, we moved to a draughty and frugally furnished vicarage in a village at the bottom of a hill near the sprawling city of Glasgow. The vicar had died, the church had been boarded up and my father had been allowed to buy the house cheap as long as he retained some sort of spiritual presence in the community. Twice a month we all sat in the icy front parlour, our noses tickling with coal dust, and took it in turns to read chapters from the Bible to three old ladies who always kept their coats on. I suspected they were deaf as posts but nodded a lot to compensate. Once when I was left alone to do the reading, I tried them on *Lady Chatterly's Lover*. They seemed to like it and reacted just as vigorously with a Hallelujah, in fact.

On the other side of the hill was a quarry and so the hill got smaller and smaller each year. When I was old enough to play on my own, I used to walk to the top—only one day there wasn't a top anymore just a sheer drop and lots of grey dust. The sound of explosions boomed through the air every day like ominous thunder. Although the noise made visitors jump, everyone who lived in the village had become so accustomed to it that we used to twitch when we couldn't hear the booms on days like bank holidays or Christmas.

Below, the River Clyde widened out from a mean little river into a wide shallow sea. But even though it looked inviting from a distance, you could never swim. There was so much rubbish floating at the edge, you'd have had to wade out through several feet of slimy crisp packets and rusty beer cans before you could even see any water.

But the hill, our side of it at least, was a long slope of coarse green bracken and soft Scotch pine with a stream at the bottom. I used to start at the top and race straight down it, stampeding through the tangling stems which slowed me like widespread arms, until I tumbled somersaults into unseen craters or fell down hidden ditches which appeared quite suddenly as if made each night by falling stars.

As for me, I suppose I was a strange looking child, thin and awkward, with fine hair, a brace on my teeth and a tendency to blush when upset. And as well as being what is known tactfully as a late developer, I was made to wear brightly coloured Crimplene dresses sewn in South Africa by women in a missionary bible class.

My father was by then a supplier of Gideon bibles to hotel rooms. On a good day he would come home and declare with obvious pleasure that five or six had been stolen. It always seemed odd that a sin could be quite so godly. Anyway, with his meagre income and strong sense of Presbyterian guilt, I was told that we were not (exactly) poor but modest. So modest that I never had many of the toys, games, or things that children usually have. If I did win any prizes in raffles or was presented with gifts, they were all hastily handed over to a charity for those less well off than us, all that is, except the ones deemed unsuitable. Please don't take this as rampant sentimental self-pity but I was only ever allowed to keep broken, damaged or incomplete toys. You, my dear, were the first perfect thing I have ever been given.

It may be hard to believe but we didn't even have a television. All we had were books. Books stacked to the ceiling and in boxes under every bed, books choked with dust and an unread smell, books stashed for later use or reference, until they rose on every side of every room in huge towers. For years I played with them when my father was out, constructing small dens or stepping-stones across shark-infested seas. Until I opened one, that is, and then I was hooked.

I should explain my parents, your grandparents, I suppose. They were nice people, I'm sure of that now. Polite, modest and thoroughly decent in a late Victorian kind of way. But as for being their offspring—if there was a choice I'm convinced that the takers would be few. They were Sunday school sweethearts who shared a passionate interest in non-fiction. I was conceived one night when my father was researching female anatomy for his Higher Biology. My mother, who was a year younger, was shouting out the Latin names from a textbook he had bought in a job lot sale of old stock from the local library.

They hadn't reached the relevant chapter on copulation and claimed that they were extremely surprised and a little shocked when my mother noticed a slight swelling in her abdomen, a few months later, which proved not to be an enlarged intestine or something unpleasantly glandular.

They gave me the book for my tenth birthday on the condition I read it in its entirety before my eleventh. Just in case.

Since they knew so much and had been so let down by their lackadaisical education, they had decided to teach me at home. Every day between nine and four, I sat at a desk in the middle of the kitchen and was taught. I do not recommend it, my dear. Not unless you want to work your way through the Encyclopaedia Britannica page by page on weekdays and Practical Accounting on Saturdays.

Like two large children, my parents inhabited a world quite of their own making. She would spend hours with her eyes detached, her body poised with tea-towel in hand, her mind so far away that I would sometimes repeat myself fifteen times, each a little louder than the last until I was eventually shouting. And then she would suddenly snap, "I heard you the first time!" I never knew where she went, to a land of European train engines or maybe a world of rare butterflies with unpronounceable names. But she was very pretty, my mother, as pretty as St Sebastian.

Occasionally, my father would come home and say one seemingly made-up word in her ear, one nonsensical utterance that would make her start laughing until she wept. But if the bibles had clearly lain untouched for months and were thick with dust and scattered with the commas of toenail clippings, he would ask politely when supper would be ready and then infer that her cooking was inedible. Which it was. And then no matter what time of day or night it happened to be, he would ask me why I wasn't in bed yet, without waiting for an answer.

My father was a neat man, the type who trimmed his nose hairs with a special pair of trimmers and wouldn't eat in candlelight because it changed the colour of the food. It's hard to describe what he looked like because when I think of him, all I see is his puzzled expression as he gazed at me looking as if he didn't recognise me but should. Do I do him an injustice? If I met him now, would I see instead the years of self-sacrifice he used to pontificate about, the toil and loathsome role as a disciplinarian, for my own sake rather than his own sadistic pleasure?

Surprisingly, despite all the books, our house was spotlessly tidy, meticulously clean, so free from dust or general mess that as soon as you placed an item of crockery on a table or sideboard, the very second that china touched polish it would be whisked away to the sink to be washed, dried and neatly placed back in its proper place before you'd even had a chance to miss it. Even now, I feel perversely comforted by the sight of a huge pile of dishes in a sink, while the sound of washing-up liquid bottles squeezed assertively still makes me jitter.

And so by the time I was thirteen what with the hill, my diminishing possessions and the vanishing teacups, I was used to life shrinking, not growing. I became obsessed with my own physical presence and developed a real fear of disappearing. Every door I passed through I slammed behind me as loudly as I could and every time I listened to the radio I turned it full blast until the air seemed to quiver. Sometimes, when my parents went out, I stole my mother's motley selection of secret make-up (father never knew her face was not all natural) and tried to draw a face into the blank white disc that reflected back at me from the bathroom mirror. I underlined my eyes, filled in my mouth a bright brick red and backcombed my hair until it rose up around my head like a straggly halo. I must have looked extremely weird, like some sort of child-hag.

No one ever saw me though. I used to sit on a large rock on my own in a stream and pretend I was a Jezebel. As for friends, I told myself I didn't want them.

One day, when I had just turned fifteen, I learnt a trick with mirrors. I won't bore you with details, but I discovered that by careful manoeuvring and by using a series of visual tricks involving the principles of the prism, I could make myself disappear and reappear somewhere else. It wasn't magic, just something I had discovered in an old copy of *Physics for Fun,* Volume Two, and adapted a little. With practice, I became more accomplished and was soon able to sneak past my parents without them having even the faintest inkling of anything untoward.

It gave me, I suppose, a new lease of life. It meant I could go out in the evening, erase myself entirely from the quiet, strange life of my parents and explore. And if my mother should ever look into my room to check up on me, I'd be there, fast asleep in my little warm bed with the light off. Or maybe I wouldn't.

At first I just walked. I began to prowl at the time of night just before dusk when the light fades. From the shelter of the bramble bushes along the Old Mill Road, I'd walk the length of the back of Heather Street, look through brightly lit kitchen windows and smell the steam of hot tea, the crisp of towels on radiators and hear the stereophonic sound of TVs all tuned to the same channel.

Back at my own house, I began to hate the Spartan surfaces, the bare bulbs, the constant chill, the perennial smell of damp washing and the sense that nothing ever happened unless it did so between two hardback covers. I longed to feel that I existed, that I could make an indelible mark somewhere or on someone. To me, the silence of minds reading books seemed to wear a hole in the air.

So one day I took the long blue train with dirty orange seats into Glasgow, my birthday money in my purse, a timetable and a clutch of my mother's make-up stuffed into my duffel coat pocket. My feet were crammed into shoes with heels so high they looked to me like two little skyscrapers. I'd bought them, surreptitiously, a month before from a church hall jumble sale that I'd been volunteered to help at. Underneath my coat I wore one of my father's old shirts so I had decided not to take my coat off, no matter what befell me and my Sunday best skirt.

The train squealed to a halt at Queen Street and I climbed off like everybody else and hurried up stairs sticky with spilt stuff and powdery cigarette ash. Once out in the street, I was blinded by the gloss of the city, by the blur of car headlights reflected in shop windows and the huge neon Golliwog that smiled its deranged smile down at the street from a rooftop. Nothing had prepared me for the noise and the bustle and I stood transfixed to a spot of pavement while people tutted and pushed past and prodded me with the spokes of their umbrellas.

I had to move or I would have been simply swept away. And so I headed across George Square at so fast a pace that the pigeons rose in flapping clouds around me. I walked and walked until my feet began to bleed. But I didn't want to acknowledge the fact that I was crippling myself with yesterday's vindictive fashion. I didn't want to discard my newly acquired grown-up swagger that made me look as if I knew where I was going when I hadn't the faintest idea. So I went into a cafe under a railway arch in which, I remember clearly, the only customers were several elderly women wearing thick make-up and fur coats, and I asked, to the obvious amusement of the man behind the counter, for the menu.

As I listened to the trains rumble overhead, I sipped a mug of milky white coffee and ate a Tunnock's teacake. Then, bolstered with sugar, I headed to a brightly lit entranceway below a large sign across the road and I joined the queue. It was a nightclub called The Eiffel.

I suppose because I could have passed for being 18 and single in a very dark room, they let me in for free. I took the linoleum-covered stairs two at a time and pushed the swing doors open into a huge hall with a curved ceiling studded with spangled musical notes. The walls were painted deep red and the seats were made of scuffed green leather. At one side was a bar stocked with a long row of bottles all filled with different coloured liquids, just like the fantastic chemistry set I once won in the Women's Guild raffle and had to donate to Children Behind Bars.

As I weighed up whether I had enough money to risk asking for a drink, I suddenly thought of my mother. I imagined her in the dove grey cardigan and grey plastic slip-on shoes she always wore standing in front of the pink mirror beside the flashing slot machine. As well as looking underdressed, she looked slightly lost, the way she usually did. It was her dissatisfied, it's-not-my-fault-expression, as in the sponge cake for the church bazaar is rock hard and is as flat as a large cowpat but if only the recipe hadn't been wrong/someone hadn't turned the cooker up too high/she hadn't been interrupted at a critical stage by a telephone call from a woman trying to sell double glazing who she hadn't the heart to be rude to, then it would have been perfect.

In the murk of the dance hall, with the occasional light flashing into my face from the spinning mirror ball above, I suddenly realised I didn't know what I was doing there all alone. A large lump welled up in my throat. I felt foolish, naive, like the time I got lost in a supermarket and hid inside the passport photo booth until my name was announced on the public address system. My mother, who had started to bite her fingernails distractedly, suddenly turned to me and said, in her usual dismissive tone: "Stop being so pathetic."

That sobered me up in an instant, I can tell you, and since she had never even set foot in a nightclub like The Eiffel, I immediately felt much older and much wiser than her. I banished the image of my mother from my mind and headed to the bar. As I wondered what I should order without giving myself away—my parents were Episcopalians and both teetotal apart from a weekly slug of communion wine—I looked over my shoulder at the dance floor. It was time, I decided with all the conviction a fifteen-year-old can muster, to find out how people live in the real world.

The nightclub was actually almost deserted. The music that boomed out of the overhead speakers had a metallic quality and bounced around the walls quite unpleasantly. It was so loud that it was almost impossible to tell if the singer's voice was deliberately warbly or if it was simply distorted. And as I had no record player, nor friends with a record collection, and was only allowed to listen to music as long as it was Bach, it wasn't surprising that the wails and shrieks, which provoked other people to mouth words and tap their feet, passed me by completely.

All around the walls were notices. No Pass outs, No Petting, No Spitting and No Severe Intoxication. In the middle of the dance floor, two bare-footed girls in wallpaper-stiff dresses jiggled around, their shoes and handbags heaped between them. Cigarettes dangled from their hands like extra fingers that had caught fire and occasionally they puffed on them and blew smoke rings at the ceiling. They may have been trying to project an image of sophisticated detachment but it was impossible not to notice the way their eyes swerved around the room and flicked towards the swing door of the entrance every time it opened.

Further along the bar, a man with the greasiest hair I had ever seen was watching them. The girls' eyes misted over when they glanced in his direction, which I thought was a little unkind considering their very obvious mission.

But there was no shortage of possibilities. Groups of men sat in dark corners with amber liquid in graceful glass columns lit up on the tables in front of them. Others stood at the edge of the dance floor, deliberating like bathers whether or not to jump into its dappled surface. Most of them were middle aged and overweight but all of them looked hungry.

My appetite, however, was not for them and so I decided to experiment with intoxication, while trying to avoid Severity. The drinks, it being mid-week, happy hour, special-offer time, were much cheaper than I had calculated. And as all cocktails were half-price, I started to spend my birthday money on those.

The barman was a small bespectacled Aberdonian who said he'd trained at the Ritz Hotel. In Bangor, he added. He seemed thrilled when I asked for the cocktail list and leaned across the bar in wet-lipped anticipation. I began with something called a Bodice Ripper, which was pale blue and came with a sparkler and a silver umbrella. It was quite delicious despite its rather unappetising colour.

I picked the next one because it was called Helen of Troy. It was pink and creamy with a strong tang of strawberry syrup. I had a real problem finishing the entire glass as it was extremely rich and rather like drinking liquid pudding, but I didn't want to appear rude.

The barman suggested he make me one of his own secret recipes, a drink which had no name but which he said was mind blowing, a drink which was the favourite of the Prince of Bavaria. His enthusiasm was contagious and so I instantly agreed. It was presented to me in a cup of pure ice instead of a glass; it was as green as marsh weed and tasted innocuously of peppermints. While the other cocktails had made me feel dizzy and slightly unsteady on my feet, this drink seemed to snap me back together again.

"Wow," I said and swallowed up the last of it just before the glass melted to a few bright green drips in my hand. "My mind is well and truly blown."

Meanwhile the taped music had stopped and a small band had shuffled on to the stage at one end of the dance-floor. They wore blue jackets with white trim and all had black hair, which they sluiced back. It soon became apparent that they only sang songs about losing babies and broken hearts and on closer inspection, I could see why. They looked patently unloved with cigarette burns and stains on their outfits and the kind of weary expressions that didn't exactly encourage you to have a good time. Nobody else seemed to think so either and the dance floor remained steadfastly empty.

Then I noticed something rather unusual. A bear had just

walked through the swing doors next to the No Spitting sign. Only it wasn't a real bear, but a large human wearing a suit with a metal cuff round his neck. The cuff had a long metal chain, the end of which was held by a man in a brightly coloured costume with a red tasselled hat. He played a triangular instrument, a balalaika, while the bear lollopped around the room giving out paper flyers.

I changed my mind very suddenly about the man with the greasy hair. As the bear passed he said something loud, incomprehensible but clearly supposed to be witty and then he nodded in my direction. The bear stopped abruptly and cocked his head to one side. And then he did something very strange, at least, being a girl of very little experience, it seemed that way to me. He pulled the chain from his companion's hand and turned 60 degrees to face me. Before I could scream or make any noise to register my outrage, the bear had picked me up, thrown me over its shoulder and had started to run. Face to face with its matted brown fur, my mouth filled up with fuzz, I quite suddenly snapped. Unconcerned and unaware of how many people had started to watch as the floor golluped along beneath my head, I kicked and screamed like a kidnap victim.

When the world suddenly righted itself, I was standing on the dance floor. Or rather I realised with a lurch, I was in the air above the dance floor. The bear was performing a slow, rather dignified dance and I, in my drunken green state, was its partner. The bear threw me up, whirled me around on its open paws and then cradled me like a lover. Its face, when I caught a glimpse, was locked in a bear-like grin with a plastic nose but with real, moist green eyes. Contrary to what you might expect, after I had got used to the roller coaster movements which shook me up inside and turned the nightclub into a black and silver blur, I began to enjoy it. Laughter welled up inside me and with each swoop and fling, each gravity-defying dive, I flew inside like a bird.

The song came to a stop and the band cantered instantly into the next without gambling on the slim chance of applause. Slowly, I slid down through furry arms until I was looking up into the bear's snout. With a grunt of effort, it pulled off its head and then I gazed into the face of a man. With thick, black hair, tied at the nape of his neck with an elastic band, the bear man looked unlike any other I had ever seen. There was his size, for a start, which was like a scaled-up version of most of the men in the dancehall. And then there were his eyes, which slanted up very slightly at the corners, his nose, long and straight and his mouth, which looked as if it had been drawn with a flourish, like old-fashioned writing. He stared at me and I stared at him until we suddenly realised instantaneously and looked away.

"You could have asked first," I shouted above the din of the band.

I didn't expect him to laugh. It wasn't meant to be funny. But I don't think he could help it. When my dance partner laughed it was as if he was being tickled. It was a bubble of something wonderful.

"The least I can say is thank you," he said with a bow.

The first time I saw the bear man, I was furious and enchanted at the same time. It wasn't just the way he looked or his laugh; it was the way he glanced at the world with half-closed eyes and a slightly amused expression.

I tried to speak, but my words stuttered and came out in the wrong order. Everything seemed suddenly to be falling forward, again and again and so I pulled off my torture shoes and sat down on the floor. It was, of course, the effects of the Bodice Ripper and the Helen of Troy and the Prince of Bavaria's favourite cocktail.

The bear man looked around the ballroom hoping, I suppose, for a friend to rush up from somewhere or other and rescue me. Everyone stared as if they'd never seen me before in their lives, which they hadn't. As I sat on the floor, I suddenly imagined what I must look like. I was severely intoxicated, extremely drunk, despicably pissed. My duffel coat was open wide and what with my make-up smudged and my tights all laddered, I must have looked not a day over the fifteen that I was. I glanced up and caught the bear man looking at me with a perturbed expression.

"I think you should go home," he shouted above the music.

It was then that I noticed that his voice had the deep rumble of a grisly and the slanted vowels of a foreigner. "No more dance. You're plenty drunk."

While I considered his suggestion, he sighed loudly, helped me to my feet, scooped up my shoes and after consulting briefly with the man in the red hat, half-carried me out of the dance-hall and very kindly accompanied me to the station round the corner where I just caught the last train home.

I don't remember much about the train journey apart from the fact that I slept most of the way and only woke up because my stop is at the end of the line. As I walked in my stocking soles with shoes in hand, up the road to the former vicarage, I wasn't scared of the rustle of bushes or the sigh of the night wind the way I used to be. Although I should have been listening for the low growl of approaching traffic, I was thinking about the bear man.

Sometimes I imagined that on the way to Queen Street as we walked through the narrow, almost midnight streets, I saw our reflection in a darkened shop window. And in the glass, I watch the couple as he leans over and kisses her. And then I feel the touch of his soft, soft lips on my mouth, inhale the secret dark smell of him and sense the thundering of his heart. But I went over and over that night so often in the next few months that I eventually wore it out, like a few frames of film burned by the light of the projector, and so eventually I couldn't distinguish between what actually took place and the dreams I had. I was witness to it all and yet I couldn't swear on the Bible to tell the whole truth, and nothing but. The likelihood, I now suspect, is that he had nothing to do with me and was highly relieved when the train doors hissed shut and he could go back to his red-tasselled friend. The nightclub closed down quite soon after. It became a disco called Katmandu's.

Anyway, I woke up the next morning at eleven o'clock. I was puzzled that nobody had woken me up since lessons usually started at nine sharp. I climbed out of bed and happened to glance at myself in my bedroom mirror. With horror, I saw that I was still fully dressed and my make-up was blotched and streaked all over my face. Both eyes were bloodshot and when I breathed into my palm I could still smell the alcohol from the night before.

That was the reason that I said so little when my parents sat me down and talked sensibly to me about what I had done and why it was wrong. I was holding my breath to contain the fumes.

My mother had been crying and clearly thought that I learned a little too much in the book they'd given me for my tenth birthday. At the time, however, I thought it would have been preferable for them to rant and rave and indulge in a little cathartic wrath, but no, they were above that particular approach. They spoke to me in the manner of a traffic warden who fines a driver parked on a double yellow line, with patience, bottled incredulity and a certain irritating smugness.

It was then that they told me that they had just confirmed in writing my place at St Cecilia's, a religious boarding school for girls in the Borders. I was to start the following week.

"Most of the girls go on missionary placements," said my father. "They open the bible in places where it has never been opened before."

"What, like hotels?" I said.

He wasn't at all amused by my flippancy. After a loaded pause, he brought out a typed sheet of paper which stated that I agreed to be locked in my bedroom with a Gideon bible stamped 'damaged,' my old potty, three days supply of oatcakes and cheddar and a plastic knife. A pen was produced and I was instructed to sign. I stared at them both in abject dismay.

But something prevented me from refusing point blank. In fact, I took the pen and signed. You see, in my other hand, screwed up in my palm into a crushed and slightly sweaty ball I still held the bear-man's flyer. And when my parents finally left me, my face scrubbed young and almost invisible again, my thoughts provisionally pure, I unclenched my fist and flattened it out on the bed.

"Valentine's Circus," it read. "You'll laugh, you'll cry, you'll enjoy. For two nights only, the world-famous circus and funfair. Come to Kelvingrove Park. And tell your friends."

I will continue in a moment but first I want to explain something. I could have gone to St Cecilia's and ended up in some far-flung place wearing a Crimplene dress, but it was just not in my fictional repertoire. My imagination had been stretched but never in that particular direction. And anyway since I was given no choice in the matter, I had no qualms in deciding that I didn't want to be carried along by another person's motivational curve so early in my own tale. As for my parents, I don't blame them. Accepting the role of diverting sub-plot is never easy. I know that now.

My sweetest daughter, I called you Little Wing because your body seemed so full of air and hope and height. I hope it didn't cause you problems at school and dread to think that you might have changed it to something predictable such as Isabel or Agatha. You see, inside me you floated around on that long blue rope and I became so accustomed to the stamp of your feet on my heart that I couldn't actually imagine you moving on, so to speak, and leaving. When you were born it was a huge surprise. It wasn't just the pain and the raw scrape of your tiny infant cry, but the fact you were so much more than the product of my over-active imagination.

Your skin is unbelievably, astoundingly and utterly new. My tiny doll, my *kokla,* my single slip, I called you Little Wing because I wanted to believe in angels. Now, I mustn't start because this is only the beginning. There, I have poured myself a drink. Your mother, my girl, probably gave you taste for gin. Blame me if you must, but always dilute generously with tonic.

I've had a rather depressing thought. I suppose what follows could be read as a bad example. I can't wish that I'd done everything differently and had a sensible life because then you would have never existed at all. You are a miracle. Remember that.

It is dark when I finish that page. I feel dizzy—spin, spin, bang. At first I wonder if she has the wrong daughter, the wrong girl. Maybe she is a deranged maniac, an impersonator, a corrupter of vulnerable minors or just a liar. I've never even tasted gin. The stars have come out above the dull haze of the city. I try to see my mother's face, fit the voice to a pair of eyes and a mouth. She must have kissed me once. I feel closer to Jupiter and Mars than her.

It's late and your block is dark apart from one blue light on the third floor and the glare of the single bulb on the landing which hasn't blown and not been replaced. And then I hear it very faintly, blowing in threads and billows like expensive fabric, a woman's voice underlined with the faint gauze of an orchestra. Opera. I am surrounded by ghosts.

I turn the next page.

Disappearing Act

Chapter two

The Disappearing

The next evening, when I'd heard the sounds of my parents going to bed, when I knew that they had scoured their teeth thoroughly with toothpaste, scrubbed themselves all over with tar soap and cold water and then climbed between the icy sheets feeling spiritually and physically pristine, I tried the door. It was locked. It has always puzzled me as to why such holy residencies should be so full of door furniture, as I believe it is known, but every room in that house had the potential to lock up secrets, mad women, tools of vice or keep the marauding heathens out.

I remember it was autumn then. My bedroom was on the first floor and right outside my window grew an old and not particularly fertile apple tree. The tree had produced a single fruit that year and I had been watching it grow and slowly ripen. That night, I threw on an extra jumper which someone religious had knitted, picked the apple and climbed down the tree. I ate it as I walked towards the train station. Unfortunately, it was not the rosy globe of fairytales but hard, green and sour. I threw it into a stream where, along with twigs and leaves and, dare I say it now, happy endings, it was swiftly carried away towards the wide, shallow water of the River Clyde.

The train's departure was delayed due to a cow on the line and by the time it had chugged into the city and I had walked from Partick station past the Kelvingrove Art Galleries and the Kelvin Hall to the park, it was long past my official bedtime. I wondered if my parents had checked up on me. But I knew that they wouldn't. 'Three days and three nights,' my father would have said, 'She is cast out into the wilderness for that time, no more no less.'

Yet a bedroom, I argued to myself, is not the same as a desert. Not by any stretch of the imagination.

It was dark when I reached the wide, wooded walkway that splits Kelvingrove Park in two. The smell of hot fat, cooking sugar and engine grease infused the air and through the black branches of ancient trees I saw coloured lights flying so fast they blurred into an exhilarating haze. A light wind blew gusts of something combustible, an alchemy of pleasure and danger and thrill.

As I came closer, I made out the shape of a big white tent with a red neon heart positioned on top. It towered over the town of little tents and caravans pitched all around it. I could hear the screech of hooters and the hysteria of pounding pop music, the sound of people screaming quite involuntarily in terror as they were spun round on the waltzers and the muffled jangle of a brass band. I reached the front gate: an ornately carved wooden archway painted in bright colours, and looked up. Huge letters gilded with flaky gold paint spelled out a single word: VALENTINES. I walked through.

The circus show in the big top had already begun and the wooden doors were closed. And yet I wasn't disappointed because there was still the funfair. Though I'd volunteered to help at summer fetes, won bottles of ginger wine and once come second in the egg and spoon race, this was quite, quite new to me.

Children ran from ride to ride, their cheeks red, their eyes as bright as marbles. Girls laughed like cartoons while their boyfriends shot tin pellets at pockmarked targets. As I clumped along the muddy make-shift streets, women wearing headscarves called me over from circular booths and asked me if I wanted to play games with hoops or balls or plastic ducks. They told me that I had a lucky face, that it was easy as pie, that just for me they'd make it three goes for fifty pence. Behind them were heaps of teddy bears, bulging bags of coloured water where goldfish darted, watches, radios, TVs and even a girl's bicycle. I said I'd come back later and I meant it.

I walked on, past booths where men spun pink sugar into sickly sweet cotton wool or turned hot dogs relentlessly on their greasy griddle. I bought a toffee apple and still remember the first snap of the hard, dark red candy and the disappointing texture of the floury flesh inside. And then I thought about the bear man.

When I heard the explosion that came from the circus tent, I was the only one in the near vicinity who didn't jump almost out of my skin. As I said, I was used to explosions. I headed towards it, my courage fuelled by adrenalin and curiosity in almost equal measure. Behind the Helter Skelter, where the grass was untrampled but littered with rubbish, I ducked under the guy ropes until I found a small open flap in the canvas big enough to crawl through. Inside the big top, the smell of sulphur and sawdust was underlined with a stronger, muskier note. I hesitated for an instant just in case anyone was watching. But there was no one; even the teenage drinkers and snoggers seldom strayed far from the main drag. Then from somewhere close-by sirens wailed once more to signal that another bout of screaming was about to begin. So without further delay, I crouched down onto my hands and knees and crawled through.

I found myself underneath a large bank of seating, completely dark apart from regularly spaced shafts of diffused light that marked the rows above. Dust motes drifted down, interspersed occasionally by the slow float of a crisp packet or sweetie wrapper.

Even before my eyes had grown accustomed to the gloom, however, I sensed that something was coming towards me from the left along the side of the tent, something big and hot and not quite human, something which was not supposed to be there. There was no time to return the way I came and so I pushed myself small against the canvas, my breath coming quicker as the thing came lumbering closer. Fear, horror and a sense of irrational foreboding took hold of me. I turned my head away as if the thing would vanish if I didn't catch sight of it. But then with low dark rumbles and deep snorts, it was suddenly there on all fours right in front of me, huge and hairy and drooling slightly.

It was a bear, my dear daughter, not a man in a suit, but a real one with a collar around its neck and a pair of black black eyes.

Of course I thought I would be eaten or bitten or at least mauled. I know that bears might look friendly but they can scoop up huge fish with their claws and have large and pointed teeth. With a gruff sneeze, the bear pushed its wet nose towards me and, before I could move an inch, nudged the open palm of my hand. I started to cry, very softly, and lifted both hands up until my palms were pressed together. The bear looked at me. I looked at the bear. It was as if time had stopped.

And then the band started playing in the circus ring again and the sound of laughter burst up above us like a rainstorm. The bear reared up on its hind legs. I gasped. I buckled. I would have screamed if all the breath hadn't been sucked right out of me already. But right there in front of me, in the underworld light with the sound of trumpets and tambourines filtering down, the bear started to dance.

From somewhere a little way off to the left a man's voice whispered sharp and urgent. "Nina," he hissed. "Nina."

The bear stopped dancing, cocked its head and listened. As a storm of applause erupted in the ring, the bear lunged down and galloped back towards the voice.

My heart raced in my chest, my palms were damp with sweat and bear spit, but I was alive. I waited until it had definitely and most certainly departed and there was no chance of a re-run and then I concentrated on breathing normally in, out, in, out, until, gradually, I managed to calm down.

Quickly, I crept back towards the gap in the canvas. I hurried faster when I heard the sound of men's voices approaching from the direction the bear had come and just managed to squeeze through in time. Once safely on the other side, I paused and listened. One of the men was apologising while the others were cursing and rattling what sounded like a chain.

I know now that the sound of the explosion was the sound of the bear trainer being fired from a cannon and that the bear had been deliberately liberated from her cage before the finale in which she was about to take part. The bear trainer was trying to make a little money on the side with an extra act for which he had no training and which eventually was the cause of his undoing, and he had carelessly left his main source of income unattended.

Anyway, none of that mattered right then. And unbeknown to me, I was witness to an abduction and escape meticulously planned out and executed by the man I'd danced with the night before. Timing as you will see, my little Wing, has always been my weak point.

Back outside in the cold October air, the panic subsided. As I wandered through the funfair, I told myself I was not dinner for a ravenous beast but a girl about to indulge in a couple of games where I might win a goldfish, a bicycle or a TV. After my stomach had been churned to the point of nausea on various speeding things, I failed to even win a key ring after ten attempts at trying to throw a ping-pong ball into a jam jar. Unlucky, said the woman with not one modicum of sympathy.

Maybe I was still in shock, maybe my subconscious was taking the lead, but when I checked in my purse for my return train fare home, I realised that I had spent every penny I had. As I walked around the funfair, not sure of what to do next, the circus doors opened and crowds of people poured out and headed towards the temporary car park. A few minutes later, the air seemed to buzz with the sound of car engines, while dozens of headlights fire-flied their way to the main road. And then, as suddenly as the sun sets in tropical countries, the funfair closed down. Blinds clanked over displays of virtually unclaimed prizes, grills cooled and hot dogs ceased their big-wheel motion. The wailing siren slowed to a moan, coloured lights blinked off in strings like the last day of Christmas, and a previously indistinguishable hum in the air suddenly stopped, making the silence of the park seem louder than ever.

Only then it was possible to hear the real sounds of the circus. Animals stamping in makeshift stalls, the creak and strain of mechanical chains on the rides, washing machines in spin-cycle plumbed into the backs of trailers, people laughing, people eating, people counting money.

My strolling nonchalance seemed ever more eccentric as the funfair switched itself off. My feet sunk deeper into the cigarette butt and hot-dog littered mud, making my pace slow and more deliberate than I would have liked. Soon I was the only one left who didn't work there and although they all pretended to ignore me, I knew that I looked suspicious.

Now I don't quite know why I did what I did next. A multitude of different factors conspired to propel me to the manager's trailer, a large, white, modern-looking caravan with a TV aerial and the lingering smell of chip fat, and knock on the door. A dog bounded up on the inside and started barking. An old woman coughed and called out. Then a man's voice asked who it was. I stuttered that he didn't know me. The door opened hesitantly and a man with dark hair, which stuck up on top, a clubfoot and a walking stick, stared out.

"Hullo. My name," I said very quickly. "Is Helena. And I'm currently available for employment."

"Sorry?" he said.

"Any jobs?"

He seemed to size me up and then exhaled loudly. Behind him in the faint blue bloom of the television set I saw a bundle of old clothes with a wrinkled face on top.

"If you're willing to start at the bottom."

"That's always the best place," I replied, "to start."

I stepped back an inch and was about to mumble that I had the wrong circus. But then the manager said very softly, "What can you do?"

I wasn't expecting this response. I was completely flummoxed, speechless in fact.

"Nothing." I replied.

He laughed and then looked me up and down again. I pulled my hands out of the cuffs of my religious jumper and tried to smile in a way that I thought could be alluring.

"Maybe," he said, "maybe."

That night I shared a tiny caravan with a middle-aged woman called Millie who told me without any enthusiasm or ceremony that she swallowed snakes and made the toffee apples. In the lull of the early morning, I couldn't sleep, not initially at least. It wasn't just the fact that Millie snored but the fact that my mind sped between two poles of action. At first I convinced myself that I had done the right thing, that I needed to see the world, to work for a living and, I tentatively told myself, to meet the bear man again. But this was swiftly replaced by a huge welling up of dread. After hours of tossing and turning, I decided that come morning-time I would accept the down-beat resolution of an education at St Cecilia's, get up before anyone else, sneak out and hitchhike home to the house on the other side of the hill from the quarry before my parents had had a chance to miss me.

When I woke at 9 A.M. I realised that the situation was now way out of my control. In the four hours in which I had finally slept, the circus people had been hard at work, dismantling the huge tent, the sideshows and the funfair, with miraculous speed. And when they had finished they had hitched up their caravans and moved on. Millie had gone and my temporary bedroom was speeding along the motorway at least 40 miles an hour to an as yet unknown destination. Like it or not, I was now a member of Valentine's Circus.

Hindsight, I now know, is never particularly constructive. In my low moments, however, I sometimes wish I had the memory of a goldfish because nothing haunts and hurts as much as if only. I never saw my parents again. I wish that I could have, if only to explain, if only to tell them that my departure was more an accident than a deliberate ploy to hurt them. But they would not have understood. And before I would even have known what hit me, I am certain I would have been shipped off on a one-way ticket to shine a godly light in the deepest, darkest destination they could think of.

At that moment, as the caravan bounced along and anything loose fell on the floor, I remember I was scared stiff and thrilled at the same time. No more tuition, I told myself, no more Encyclopaedia Britannica or readings from the Gideon Bible, no more chance of an uncertain fate under the threat of diseases borne by mosquito. I had no common sense, I see from here, just a lot of rather pointless bravado.

The circus convoy bumped its way slowly into a large field near an airport at around teatime. It positioned itself into a lop-sided circle with a clearing in the middle, and stopped.

I stepped out of Millie's caravan and took a walk around the encampment. At first I was sure I would be approached and asked what I was doing, but everyone was too busy to care who I was or where I had come from. I watched men with backs as brown as envelopes and ink blue tattoos, hoist up the big wheel and re-assemble the big top. They spoke slow, stilted English as they heaved oily black rope and hammered metal pegs into the soft brown earth. At one end of the encampment there was a cluster of old wooden trailers, which rocked with the snorts and shuffles of the animals. Through the slats I made out horses, ponies, dogs and one rather weary looking elephant, but no bear. For, as I was soon to discover, both the bear man and Nina, the bear, were gone.

Chapter three

Valentine's Circus

Well that was the beginning, the early chapters of my life.
I must admit I had absolutely no previous intention of working on a travelling circus and funfair. That was quite beyond even my wildest expectations. And as if to show my complete lack of mental preparation, I looked like I had absconded from a school trip. But since I was there and I couldn't imagine how I could get away without major humiliation involving a phone call to my parents who still, I was sure, believed I was locked in my room eating oatcakes and cheddar, I decided that I would give it a try.

I found the manager sitting on the wooden steps of his trailer staring into the distance. I turned and saw the lights from the runway had drawn red lines on horizon. A plane took off and hurtled up into the blue sky. It looked so easy.

The television still blurted and laughed inside and I had to clear my throat twice before the manager noticed me. And when he did, I could tell by his face that he was wondering what on earth had possessed him to offer me a job. After he had asked my name again and told me rather coldly that pay was £10 a week, payable on a Sunday morning in cash, he instructed me to go to the Pluck a Duck and say that Milo had sent me.

"Milo?" I said.

"Milo," he said. "That is my name. Milo Valentine."

For a few seconds, I gazed at him. But I remember, when he noticed, how vividly he stared back. And then he looked away and carefully lit the end of a large and pungently scented cigar.

"You know," he said softly. "I knew you would come."

A tiny shiver raced down the back of my neck.

"What do you mean?" I said.

He paused, took a series of small puffs and his face disappeared in a cloud as he exhaled. I waited with drumming heart until the blue smoke had cleared. And when it did, his eyes were much narrower than they had been before.

"In every town," he continued, "a girl like you appears at my door. Like clockwork."

"And what happened to them all?" I asked.

"Most of them are still here. One makes popcorn, another sells the programs, and a third, yes, she's very good. She is sawn in half every night."

I guffawed, and then covered my mouth with my hand. He took another couple of puffs.

"Others," he continued, "they come and go again. And you?"

"It depends," I said quietly. "I mean, I've come. So I'll stay."

We smiled at each other, with the insincere politeness of complete strangers as they size each other up. Then he suddenly asked me to wait, clomped up the stairs and came back a few minutes later with a small pile of clothes.

"Get out of that stuff," he said. "You look no more than fifteen. These should be about the right size."

"But I'm eighteen," I replied, too rapidly to be true.

"Sure," he said.

I felt my face blush and burn. But I would not look away. Not there, not then.

He paused.

"Be patient," he said. "And very soon we shall try you out on something more interesting. In the ring."

As I wondered what exactly he meant, a large black car turned off the main road and started to approach the circus campsite. It bounced over the grass with its engine revving and tyres splattering mud in arcs before it came to a skidding halt just in front of us.

I heard Milo Valentine sigh very softly. He stood on his steps with his dog barking, his hair all sticking out and built-up foot tapping as a woman climbed out of the driving seat. And then I watched as his face suddenly softened.

Clara must have been in her late thirties then. With black bobbed hair as shiny as a spool of fuse wire, dark red lipstick and a short black coat, which didn't hang so much as fall from the curve of her shoulders, she was quite the most stunning woman I had ever seen. A real live Jezebel.

She slammed the car door so hard it almost fell off and gave Milo Valentine a long languorous look, a smouldering glance. And then she opened the car boot and started to unpack paper bag after paper bag until she splayed out at the sides like an angel whose wings have dropped several feet.

I was suddenly aware that they were both aware that I was still standing there. And so before they had the chance to tell me politely to get lost, I mumbled my gratitude, turned hastily and half walked, half-ran back to the sanctity of Millie's caravan where I locked the door behind me and sank down on to the floor.

The clothes that Milo had given me, despite being extremely creased, were not the kind of clothes I had ever worn before. I guessed they were exquisitely, expensively, retrospectively fashionable. I held them to my face and sniffed. They smelled of scent and tissue paper; sunshine and swimming pools; they smelled of money. There was a pair of navy blue trousers made of soft cotton velvet, a red cashmere t-shirt which still bore a price tag, a short black silk cardigan with unevenly spaced buttons and a heavy floor-length woollen blue coat embroidered at the cuff with tiny shell beads.

Before I tried them on, I cut out the labels and threw them in the bin. Then I rather regretfully unpicked all the beads and the unevenly spaced buttons, just in case, for I could guess whom the clothes had once belonged to. Finally I pulled on my new outfit, closed my eyes and sighed out loud. They were the first clothes I'd ever had that actually fitted me—my mother always bought the next size up out of habit. Although Clara was almost 20 years older, her figure was roughly the same proportions as mine. While I was simply flat-chested, however, she was matchstick thin. A strange sensation tingled through me from my toes to the top of my head. It was, I suppose, a realisation that I had arrived in a story, even if at that moment I suspected that I had only been granted a walk-on, spear-holder type part.

One of the many things that I soon learned at Valentine's circus, however, was that some people never give without the promise of a return. Milo had given me his wife Clara's cast-offs, banking on the fact that she had so many she would never notice that a few were missing, as some sort of advance.

I wore the clothes day after day in the rain, the mud, the snow and the sun until they faded and changed shape, until they were unrecognisable, until they became just an extension of the me I had become. But still when Clara saw me, she'd look me over as if I had something that belonged to her. And I did. Eventually, in more ways than one.

Free gifts were an anathema at Valentine's. Nothing was free, nothing was freely given. Nothing whatsoever. On my first day as an employee I was taught how to set up plastic ducks so the ones with the winning numbers were just out of reach of the hooking pole. I was also instructed to give out plastic key rings, sets of miniature playing cards and novelty pencil tops as prizes only in special cases, such as if someone with especially long arms or a policeman happened to play. The other prizes were actually stapled or glued to a board for easy installation and removal. Of course, the girl's bike was so old it had gone rusty.

"What do you expect for 50p?" said Millie when I asked her why nobody ever complained.

"Everybody knows, but when they see those prizes, their eyes get bigger than their brains. Serves them bloody right."

It was the same story on every single one of the side shows and in time, I worked them all. The Hoopaloop used magnets to make sure that only the very strong or those who invoked a freak accident could overcome the powerful force of opposite ions and win an ancient coconut. The Balls in Bowls, where the ping pong balls were provided, had a 1:50 chance of bouncing into the deceptively small mouths of the right-size of goldfish bowl, and the fish that the lucky few won were rejects from the pet shop and would die of some vile fungus infection anyway. Only at the Prize Bingo was it possible to win, but the prizes were so undesirable that I was always surprised that anyone wanted to play at all. As I called out the numbers, I watched incredulously as streams of old ladies spent pound after pound in the hope of winning a box of mildewed biscuits or a tea towel with a photograph of Edinburgh Castle printed squint. And that was not all, not by a long way. The fairground's philosophy, if you could call it that, was based on the scam, the swindle and the notion that people were instinctively Pavlovian. There was never any short-changing or men with three tumblers and a pea, but a slightly more subtle manipulation, based around the public's almost ubiquitous faith in their own personal mixture of talent and luck. It was the proximity to the circus and its contagious sense of excitement that coated the funfair with the glitter and highly intoxicating sparkle of hocus-pocus. Just to reinforce this, a few of the older women often peered into customers' hands when they handed over their warm fifty pence pieces. But they would not divulge what they saw, not then anyway. Later they might comment on a particularly sweaty palm or a woman with unusually large thumbs.

During the day, the place looked dingy, the bright colours of the fairground as scuffed as second hand toys. Daylight revealed the bruises underneath the toffee on the toffee apples, the grit in the candyfloss machine, the oil on the seats of the Hairy Spider ride and the dust that had collected in the slot machine winnings collection tray. But **at** night, with its fairy lights, mirrors, spinning globes and delicious smells, the funfair was the kind of place where the gullible believed that magic could happen.

I became used to people's faces flushed with thrill as the silver in their pockets poured into ours quite out of its own accord. I became used to seeing grown men fall down in drunken stupors after drinking watered down beer.

Of course, if you hadn't already guessed, the bear man never came back. When I asked, I was told that he had stolen Nina, the dancing bear, and driven off in his Lada. People speculated that he had fled to Newcastle, dressed the bear up as his grandmother and then bribed everyone he met on the ferry to the hook of Holland with bottles of Russian vodka to get round the legalities of transporting animals. It seemed a little unlikely. No one had any idea why he had taken Nina, a rather bad-tempered grisly, and the bear trainer reluctantly had to turn his talents to a small troop of performing French poodles which someone had bequested in North Berwick. He swore if he ever saw the bear man again, he would slice off his head with a sabre.

Although he was part of the reason I had come in the first place, it wasn't long before I pushed him to the back of my mind. I didn't forget him, but the world I had fallen into preoccupied my every waking second. Travelling shows, as you might already know, are shifting communities that can look deceptively flimsy from the outside. In fact, most are built like a fortress with a hierarchy as steep and treacherous as perimeter stonewalls. In this particular set up, Clara was the queen of Valentine, and Milo was her long-suffering King.

She, as I had previously witnessed, was a shopaholic, a woman made almost mentally ill by a pattern of desire, purchase, and then guilt. I soon noticed the telltale swings in her moods; the elation before a day's shopping, then her absence and the return buoyant with false cheerfulness and a dozen bags. There was a certain kind of silence around her trailer while she raked through her brand new clothes, shoes, handbags and jewellery inside, trying them on in different combinations with a cigarette in her hand and a fresh drink. It was a citrus taste in the air, the sound of breath being held.

It never lasted long. Her muffled wails would mark the eventual come-down, the disappointment and dismay when it dawned on her that she felt no better, no more attractive, no more special than before. The night after a shopping trip everyone was subdued. Clara's voice would rail Milo relentlessly until he snapped, the slam of his trailer door signalling to all to get inside or keep out of his way unless they wanted to be fired on the spot or sent to shovel camel shit.

The next morning Clara would appear pale-faced and tight-lipped. She would sometimes jump back in her car with bags spilling crumpled tissue paper in an attempt to put things right. But everyone knew that these missions were usually in vain. Few returned her money and there was no point in accepting a credit note as the circus would move on and by the time she returned to that particular shop, the likelihood would be that it would have shut down. And so she made herself wear a new outfit every day and would walk round Valentine's in all weather dressed in quite ridiculous get-ups as if it were a Paris catwalk in July.

It was rumoured that she spent thousands of pounds at a time. And when Milo complained, it was said she threatened to leave him and settle down somewhere suburban. But it was obvious to all that Clara would never leave the circus. She might rage at the mud and the mess and the movement, but it was her only home. Besides, Clara was the best performer in Valentine's, with a body as supple and taut as a piece of willow and an act that was never the same twice.

Clara had trained as a ballerina at the Bolshoi in Moscow and had tried to defect to the West on her first British tour when she had just turned 17. Milo had discovered her hiding on the cross channel ferry where she had been going back and forth for six days. The circumstances varied depending who recounted them, but included hiding in a cargo crate with an elephant and love at first sight through an ex-ray machine in the large animals' enclosure. It helped that Milo, who was returning with the said elephant, spoke Russian. His mother had been born in Archangel and had learned the language from a wet nurse who travelled with the circus all over the Russian sub-continent. And so Milo whispered reassurance as Clara hid in a hay bail and those reassurances grew increasingly intimate as he smuggled her past officials and through customs. By the time they reached dry land he had proposed in Russian baby talk. How could she refuse him, Clara would ask with a vague smile, when he called her his *kokla*, his little doll. They were married the next day in Dover and honeymooned in Devon with the elephant in tow.

While Milo dealt with the money, the management and the organisation of the show, Clara worked on her stunning act, the décor, and insisted she be consulted on every aspect of the design, down to the flyers. Everybody was wary of Milo and would stop talking when they heard the soft shuffle of his clubfoot, but the whole circus, the funfair and even some of the audience, were absolutely terrified of Clara. It was something about her manner. Dressed up to the nines, she could be as docile and sweet as a domestic pet one moment, and as viscous and dangerous as a wild animal the next. A kind word gave one hope that she liked you but the very next moment, her agitated shriek would dash it.

When you saw her in the ring, and took in her grace, her dexterity and the dying swan sadness of her face, however, you knew that she couldn't help the way she was. If she had only stayed on at the Bolshoi, it was patently obvious that she would have been world-famous. Instead she was stuck like a piece of chewing gum on the bottom of a train seat on the Glasgow Underground, destined to go round and round the same piece of track forever.

They had no friends, just people they would or would not tolerate, depending on the circumstances, and no confidantes, just employees. Below them, there was a fierce and constant battle for position. Near the top of the pile were the main performers followed by the less important acts, the orchestra and the animal carers, then the funfair workers and at the very bottom, the manuals. But it all reshuffled slightly every few months as people were promoted, allegiances shifted, battles raged and acts of revenge toppled even the highest climber.

Much of it happened in the circus tent. For this was no ordinary show with safety nets, elderly convivial clowns, balloon animals and sweeties for children. In the ring of Valentine's, the acts continually evolved until they pushed the very limits of what human or animal could do. It was a place of glory or abject failure, euphoria or social exclusion and of physical artistry or terrible injury. The high-wire stunts were ambitious and incredibly dangerous, the female acts had to feature bare flesh and flashes of erogenous zones and the animals were required by the management to retain all their teeth or fangs. New tricks involving fire, weapons, explosions and a high degree of personal risk were encouraged and placed in the prime slot, at the end of the first act.

I shudder to think of it now, but dreadful things happened. Fires blazed out of control, knifes flew into flesh, bones were broken when trapeze bars snapped from their ropes and animals, half-crazy with starvation, bit or sometimes trampled their trainers. And every time that something unthinkable would take place, the band would start to play, Dolly the clown would rush into the ring, surreptitiously kick sawdust over the blood and carry the injured party away in his brightly painted wheelbarrow while the audience, partly to relieve the tension and partly because they believed it to be part of the act, laughed out loud.

Many did not survive. One of the quite beautiful Tobermory twins killed her sister with her gold lamé suspender belt as she dangled from the wheels of a flying Morris Minor. Mr Mountain, the huge Hungarian, deliberately missed the bottle of Rum that he had placed upon his wife's too-generous bosom and shot her in the heart, splattering what he thought was her adulteress blood all over a disabled school group in the front row. And Marco, the handsome young monocyclist who clearly had his eye on Clara, was fatally bitten by an adder which he had been persuaded to incorporate into his act as 'the wriggling cravat.'

But at first, I knew nothing of this. I was at the very bottom of the pile, billed to sleep in a caravan at the perimeter of the camp and called 'you girl' by any circus performer who wanted me to run some errand or other for them. I became part of the underclass, a lowly funfair worker, the Pluck a Duck girl. As I was one of many, however, like any disadvantaged group I began to feel a sense of solidarity and converse with others on my level: Lydia, the Mexican programme seller and pony-groom with her huge brown eyes, one of which was made of glass, Helmut, the East German flyer-poster and tent rigger who would sail off on his bicycle with a bag of posters over his shoulder and always come back with a few carrots for the horses and a bar of chocolate for me, and Frank, the ancient, mute snake charmer who no-one knew where he was from since he had lost his voice many years before, but who taught me how to play poker using sign language. These became the first good friends I had ever had.

Even now as I write, I can hear the Great Barrissimo singing Puccini. Elsie, his wife who takes the tickets, is cooking pasta. Every night I leave you where I know you'll be found in the morning. Every night I put out the brown manila envelope that contains your personal papers and a set of clean clothes. Every night I kiss your little head goodbye. But even though I know that Elsie and the Great Barrissimo will love you like their own, I cannot really imagine being apart from you. Not really.

Reading makes me an insomniac. I am not tired, just one more page, just one more line. My mother's words lead me through the night until they jumble together and make no sense. I don't understand anything anymore.

When I wake up, the light is not too sure that it is day and says shall I, shall I? Everything looks different at this time in the morning, as if it is reflected backwards in a mirror. The shadows fall the wrong way and make the tower blocks look as if they are about to fall over. I am a ten o'clock breakfast type of girl, not a 6.55 A.M. by the light of my radio clock. And still my mother's voice echoes through my head, clang, clang, clang, like a car alarm.

At first I don't realise it, but then I touch my face and find that it is as damp as the bathroom walls. My dreams leave condensation on me, sometimes. I dreamt of Elsie, big soft warm Elsie with her smell of cardigans and her way of touching my hair, STOPIT, and the angel hair spaghetti, which she made me for my birthday. Honey pie, silly bun, golden girl, little pet. I am not a pet, a pet is a dog or a cat and I am not that, dumbo, and no, I don't want a cuddle.

We are opposites, my mother and I. You can see how independent I am. From miles away, you can see it. I've always been like this. I could walk when I was 9 months old, read when I was two, cook when I was five, wash and iron my own clothes when I was seven and I had a bank account when I was eight. It says Miss Wing Plum on my chequebook. I made up my surname, since I didn't want to be called Heliotrope, a stupid name. And as for Ringling... let her explain.

What does she know anyway? It's different for children and young people nowadays. We have rights, we are noticed, and we can phone up numbers for free and speak to strangers and tell them things about our parents or guardians in perfect confidence. I often wanted to do it, but didn't know where to start. And besides, I never needed parents, or brothers or sisters. What for? What for when guardian doesn't mean guardian angel and who wants a mother when you could end up with one like mine. No thank you.

A large grey van with the words Randy's Budget Removals has just pulled into the empty car park below. Three huge men and one skinny one get out. Somebody is moving. Somebody is leaving. Your light is on. Not you. Oh please let it not be you. But no, they come to my block. Now you're standing at your window. Are you worried that it's me?

I exercise all morning, stretching and pulling and hanging while counting to one hundred. But still my legs will not do the things I tell them to. They have grown longer in the night. They stretch like elastic.

I hide my mother's manuscript. Julie would want to read it and then ask me questions in an attempt to unravel my psyche. When she found the copy of *Little Women* which the previous tenant had left in the meter cupboard and which I was about to burn because I hated it so much, she went on for months. It was unbearable.

I have marked the page. It is my inheritance after all.

She is forty seconds late, out of breath and carrying a tin of pickled mussels. This annoys me for mussels are not the same as oysters. And smoked is not the same as pickled. To make matters worse, a man follows her in. He is a grown man with a pair of metal frame spectacles and a red and blue nylon anorak.

"Who the hell is he?" I shout.

But he doesn't stop, he doesn't hesitate for one single second but walks right into my living room carrying a stupid fold-up wheel chair and smiling a fatuous smile.

"Hello," he says as if he is surprised to see me. And then he sits down with a loud thump on my sofa.

"This is my husband, Graham," Julie says.

"Well pleased to meet you. Now please bugger off, Graham," I say.

They both laugh and I wonder if I am hallucinating. Graham's laugh is so loud it makes my fingernails hurt.

"We're treating you to tea," says Julie, her eyes flicking up at me from the visual sanctuary of the swirly carpet. "Graham's taken the day off work, a holiday, in fact. So don't be like that."

And now I see. I'm supposed to be grateful.

"We thought we'd drive you to the sheltered housing, just for a look and then take you to our favourite cafe in the shopping centre. They do a wonderful fly cemetery."

"No," I say. "I'm not going anywhere. Not now, not ever. And I would never eat anything with flies in it."

48

She sighs and looks at Graham.

"It's a kind of cake," he says. "Made with raisins. They look just like flies."

Then he shrugs and blows his nose in one long snort on a screwed up piece of pink lavatory paper. I suddenly feel sorry for her, being married to a man like that; one who comes with enough sound effects to drive you insane.

"For me then?" she says softly. "We've hired the chair specially and everything."

And then she strokes my hair, the way that Elsie used to.

I am wearing my dark glasses, a black hat, black gloves, a black scarf, a black coat and am covered with a large green tartan blanket (Julie's). For once in what must be months, the lift actually works. So we descend in the piss-stinking, graffiti-sprawled metal box with all the numbers of the floors scored out until we hit the ground floor with a thump which makes Graham project a nasty lurching sound from somewhere near the back of his throat.

Outside, the air smells, I mean it really stinks, of cats and rubbish. It is far worse than I ever could have imagined. The feeling of the pavement under the wheel chair wheels gives me the opposite of vertigo and I try not to breathe, try not to let any down-there-air into my mouth. Julie and Graham have a large red car, which pongs of air freshener. I wonder which is worse. Inside or out. There is nobody about. Nobody. Nobody to see me being taken away to an unknown destination in the back of a Ford Mondeo. I want to weep but don't want to give them the satisfaction of a spontaneous emotional outburst.

We drive for twenty minutes along a motorway and pull off through a large gateway with a red triangle sign and two stooped people on it. Julie is a nervous driver and brakes violently every time she approaches a sleeping policeman. Personally, if I could drive, I'd accelerate. All around us are little houses made of concrete pretending to be gingerbread. They have sloping roofs and **twee** wooden doorways with tiny strips of bright green grass in front. We stop at 144b and after a palaver with the chair where it tries to fold up with me inside it, Graham pushes me along the concrete path. As Julie fumbles with the key, I look at the large flowerpot that flanks the porch. It is full of flowers, large red flowers.

"Aren't they lovely," says Julie. "Winter carnations."

I reach over and touch one. It is slimy and slightly dusty. I pull not very hard and it comes out in my hand. It is made of plastic.

"Oh," says Julie. "You'd better stick it back in."

The flat smells of boiled things. They push me into the living room and leave me in front of a TV that isn't switched on. I notice that every doorway has large gilt handles.

"There's a microwave," says Julie from another room. "And an electric blanket. And a Teasmaid."

"A heated towel rail," says Graham as he clumps around. "A surround shower, double glazing."

Everything in the room is the same shade of beige. A few cigarette holes in the carpet and a worn patch on one side of the sofa are the only evidence of the last resident. There is a large sign on the wall. I take off my sunglasses and push myself a little nearer. It says. "No cooking, no alterations to the decor, no visitors except by prior arrangement, no fires, no removal of flowers (changed quarterly), no smoking, no drinking, no loud music and all residents must note that if they are late for meals, the management cannot be held responsible."

Julie throws herself down on the sofa. It makes a crunching, sliding sound as if there is polythene beneath the covers and hardboard beneath that. Graham hovers at the doorway breathing like an old Hoover.

"Well?" she says.

"Who else lives here?" I ask.

"Lots of people," she says.

"Who?" I repeat.

"Um… people with disabilities," she says in a sing-song voice. "People who need a little help to fit into the community, people who are in some way challenged, you know, all sorts of things from mild to the more severe problems."

I look up at the ceiling. It is covered with spongy tiles. It doesn't look strong enough for my rings. And then I notice a small black lens above the curtain rail with a blinking red eye.

"What's that?" I say.

Julie looks a little embarrassed. She looks at Graham. He starts to whistle. How can she stand him?

"It's just to make sure you're okay," she says. "They don't like to intrude with people knocking on the door all the time."

There is an awkward silence filled sporadically with Graham's nasal whistle.

"They organise trips," says Julie eventually. "To the seaside, to the pantomime, to the shopping centre. In fact, I think they're there today, singing carols for charity."

"It feels like a coffin," I say. "This room smells of death. Has somebody died in here?"

"Look," says Julie, standing up. "It was up to you. We tried everything—therapy, drugs, physio—but you didn't respond. You didn't try, did you? You wouldn't go to group sessions, you refused to go to the hospital for tests or take the correct medication. It took a lot of work to get you in here. You're very lucky in fact."

I feel tears start to well up in my eyes. I push my sunglasses back on and the room looks like it's made out of fake mahogany.

"I'll die too if I come here," I say.

"Rubbish," says Julie.

The shopping centre is back along the motorway, past a large factory and over the canal. I've seen it from my flat, the large carpet of different coloured cars and the grey building that squats in the middle. Inside, although it is still November, Christmas has arrived. Tinsel and complicated metallic decorations rustle in the air conditioning. The light is sort of middle of the day bright with spotlights of blinding summer on shop windows. In the air is a smell, a smell of freshly baked cakes that, if I deduce correctly, is being wafted through ducts in the skirting.

The people inside all seem to be wearing coloured anoraks, like Graham, or have steamed up spectacles like Julie. They push babies in buggies that demand things, their high-pitched voices screaming to stop, stop at that shop or grannies in wheel chairs that gaze sadly at me from the same level as we pass like boats on an artificial lake. I ignore them of course. Others with cigarettes in their mouths and piles of bags at their feet, sit on the edge of pools of green water full of ten pence pieces looking depressed. But most, their eyes fixed at near focus, glide from window to window or from Low Prices, Sale Ends Today and Bargains Galore signs. It is hell. Shopping hell.

Graham slides me up to a table in a small cafe, which opens on to the main concourse, and I'm glad he let Julie drive their car. Everybody seems to be eating but still they look hungry. Somewhere out of sight is a choir signing along badly to a tape recording of Christmas Carols.

And then I see you, slowly coming towards me in your grey moth-eaten coat and your Russian fur hat. Your colours, like mine, look alien in the primary shades that surround us. You are wearing earphones and listening to music. Close up I see your face has a sort of northern quality, with crags and overhangs and ice green slashes for eyes. It is not a beautiful face, but one that thinks.

You don't recognise me. Why should you? I look about 103. A small distance behind you are two security guards. I wonder what you've done.

I am half way through a cake—too sweet, too big, probably too expensive—when I long to get out of that place, I long to breathe new air and get away from the artificial daylight, to stop hearing that beastly loop of *Silent Night, Do They Know It's Christmas Time* and *Little Donkey* repeated over and over again. I am tired of Julie and Graham, tired of their chatter about the price of festivities and the sale at the DIY store, tired of being bombarded with sounds and smells and sights which ask me to react, tired of sitting there immobile in a chair with wheels. But most of all, I want to be on my own again, I want to get back to the manuscript.

Julie and Graham agree it's time to go. They have to. I smash three cups and saucers, leaving a spill of greasy coffee whitened with fake milk and splintered china all over the floor and am just about to start on the plates when Graham hastily takes off the brake and pushes me to the nearest exit. I like the silence as we pass. The people look like they have woken up at last.

Outside it is dark and wet, the way it should be on a November evening at 5.30 P.M.

"I'm sorry," I say to Julie and Graham as we reach floor 36. The lift has broken again and they have had to carry me up the stairs. Their faces are both bright red and Graham gasps so loudly and regularly he sounds like the industrial revolution. I smile angelically.

"Oh Wing," says Julie when she gets her breath back, and I can see that she wants to say things that would only be inappropriate.

Later, much later, when I have shaken all traces of their presence out of my mind, I sit and listen to your music. It drowns out the police sirens and the lonely wail of the dockyards. My mother's manuscript smells of sour milk and yew trees and lies on my lap in front of me. A band of light reflected from your window falls across me in one single yellow stripe.

Chapter four

The Levitation of Love

British Geography is not my strongest subject. Although I have a thorough knowledge of Albania, Bolivia and China, I never reached England in *Countries of the World,* Volume One. After twelve months with Valentine's, I stopped noticing where we were. We travelled for miles all over Britain and across the Irish Sea but, as I'm sure you'll know, once you become accustomed to the constant motion of migration from one place to another, the world becomes a backdrop with strange names and incomprehensible accents which one simply moves through.

Anyway, at that point I was not entirely lost. I thought of my parents sometimes and sent them a postcard from Blackpool to say that I was well and happy and to tell them that I would come back soon. I did intend to at a later date because, to tell the truth, I was homesick. Sometimes I sniffed the religious jumper searching for a last trace of them. But if there was anything vaguely virtuous left in its purls and plains, it had been quickly superseded by the pungent infusions of the funfair.

Girls like me, joined, and girls, unlike me, left. Eventually, I bought some new, much cheaper clothes and learned how to apply make-up without looking like a teenage reprobate. I grew, I suppose, not taller or wider or more voluptuous, but into what I thought I could be. Although the occasional shadow of the mouse of the girl I had been must have been obvious, I eventually acknowledged that I was prettier than most, if still a little raw at the seams.

And people began to notice. Millie, her hands sticky with toffee apple, once chastised me for talking for too long to a group of local boys, one of whom won a goldfish. But they spent fifteen pounds, I told her. And besides, she was wrong to think I would cast my net so casually.

With the manner of the desired, which I had only borrowed, I hasten to add, not adopted whole, I deflected men's glances with sheer disinterest and ignored their comments as if they were the utterances of a lower species. The Wall of Death rider tried to kiss me one night but I turned him down politely. The very next day he had a terrible accident involving an inebriated spectator, which made me feel a little guilty even though I was not in the least bit responsible. Although I had no real confidence, I knew I was bound for more than a speedy snog behind the hot dog stand.

I was biding my time. I told myself I'd meet the bear man again, I just didn't know when or how. And so every night I washed my nonchalant fairground persona away, removing the black and red streaks of lipstick and mascara with cotton wool to reveal the blank where a face I should have recognized should have been.

But once I had mastered the job, I became restless. I became bored. Time dragged, slowing me down and making each day feel like it would never end. Sometimes as I collected warm 50ps from the hands of over-excited teenagers, I seriously believed that I would never feel the way they did ever again. And when they lost, as I knew they would, I wanted to tell them that winning is a matter of degree.

When Milo eventually summoned me, I had my own caravan, inherited from Marco, the fatally snake-bitten mono-cyclist. It wasn't particularly comfortable and if I remember correctly, leaked in bad weather, but it was still my very own space, a few square feet of calm infused with the smell of bicycle grease.

It was pouring with heavy winter rain that day, the kind that blows sideways in large wet drops and soaks you from every angle it can. I was sitting in my caravan drinking tea with the other funfair girls as water dripped around us into saucepans. Someone was talking about how much Clara had just spent on shoes, when there was a loud and authoritative knock on the door. Dolly, the clown, stood outside, holding the large plastic see-through umbrella that he used in his act. He wasn't smiling, not even his greasepaint.

"Milo wants to see you," he said.

"What is it?" said my tea-drinking companions crowding around the door.

"That's for Milo to know and the girl to find out," said Dolly with a rather unpleasant leer. "Shouldn't you be setting up?"

I had actually forgotten the promise he had made me many months before and had no idea why he had summoned me. Not a clue. And so I put on my coat and followed Dolly along the wooden gangplank that spanned half an acre of puddle and fresh mud, and ducked under a flap and into the ring. I had only been there twice since the day I joined Valentine's. But the smell of sawdust and damp rope, of wild animal and fear, brought back the first night I had arrived at Valentine's. I suddenly remembered the dark mass of bear dancing under the seats to the sound of the brass band, and the roars of laughter that sprinkled down intermittently from above.

At first I thought the big top was empty. I listened to the thrum of the rain on the canvas and noticed how different in tone it was from the sound of rain on the caravan roof and how much, in contrast, I preferred it. And then, as it often did in winter due to a temperamental connection, the generator's hum stopped with a jolt. The lights flickered and went out, shouts rose up from outside and somewhere far away a horse complained.

I waited. Nothing happened. I dared not move an inch. It was as if I had been wrapped up in thick black velvet or dropped into a pot of pitch. I started to sing, just to make sure I hadn't died or become paralysed or something dreadful and hadn't realised it. I don't have a strong voice, not one with the warble of the professional, but it is clear and pure and can stay in tune. I think I sang something my mother had taught me, something like 'Jesus, Clean my Soul.' Then, as suddenly as it stopped, the generator coughed and started up again. A small cheer rose up from outside and, one by one, the bulbs strung around the tent poles re-illuminated.

In the new light I saw that I was not alone after all. Milo Valentine was sitting in the back row of the bank of seats, his clubfoot resting on the chair back in front, his stick held like a barrier across his lap.

"Oh," I said. "I'm sorry."

"What for?" he said. "That was very... sweet."

I couldn't meet his eye. I suddenly wanted to laugh. There was nothing funny about the situation but I think down deep I was scared, scared of what was happening, scared of what was about to happen and scared of the consequences.

"Come here," he said. "I have something I want to say to you."

Of course, he told me that I was the most beautiful girl he had ever set eyes on, he told me it was time, time for me to shine at last, he told me that I had the talent to be a huge success. But as I am sure you can guess, it was more than an offer of promotion, much more. With one step I could jump from the bottom straight up to the top. For that I would have done anything he asked. And he knew it.

Milo and I met in the long slow lunch times when Clara was out shopping and everybody else was resting. We practiced for four weeks before he was happy. What do I remember of it now? A strange sensation of levitation and youthful certainty that only other people fell.

My spot was to be the dreaded last in the first act. I was to wear a dark blue outfit with silver stars and gold spangles, which covered my breasts and fell into a small skirt. On my back Milo pinned a pair of bronze lamé wings. I didn't ask whom the costume used to belong to and didn't dwell for too long on a curious stain half way down the left side.

I was suspended from the ceiling on a flaming paper horse and, since I had no training or acrobatic skill, simply stood up, sang *You Only Live Twice,* performed a few minor moves and then dived from the burning prop into a small pool that had been specially constructed. I started about ten feet from the ground, but Milo pulled me higher and higher each time until I was eventually at least thirty feet above the ring.

It was hugely dangerous, an act of sheer folly, I now admit. If the pool were just a couple of inches out of place I would dash myself against the sides and be prone to hideous injury and if the horse burned too fast and I lost my nerve I would catch fire and be scorched alive. Every time I jumped I could have smashed my skull against the bottom or ended up with a broken neck. But I was never frightened. Not once. Looking back, compared to the other activity I was engaged in, my act, however ridiculous this sounds, was almost safe.

After that winter day in the big top when the rain made us feel like we were as alone as Noah, Milo and I became lovers. I liked to think at the time that it was spontaneous, an act of unrestrainable passion. But now I wonder if I ever had a choice.

Within hours, my caravan was hauled across the mud to be nearer those of the other performers', my name was added in miniscule letters to the circus leaflets and I was even granted my own mailbox despite the fact that in all the time I had been there, I had never received a single letter.

As I gravitated ever closer to the cool red heart at the centre of Valentine's, I left my old friends behind. That was the way it had to be at Valentine's and they knew it too.

Others replaced them: the trapeze girls with their long false eyelashes, fake tans and hideous scars, the ringmaster who pretended to be French aristocracy and who gave me a very ancient bottle of Chanel No. 5 for Christmas, and Dolly the Clown who started invit-

ing me to his select post-show gatherings to which Milo would come
once he'd counted the takings.

Did I tell you that I am addicted to the smell of your skin at
the back of your neck, to the brand new scent of your head? You
never notice how beautiful your own skin is when you are young.
You never see the way it glows and smoothes like something gift-
wrapped with moonlight. Not then, not ever. You only notice years
and years later when suddenly, or so it seems, your baby skin has
been stolen and been replaced by another layer much closer in texture to old handbags.

Milo must have been at least forty and used to spend ages
touching my skin, as if were the most precious silk in the world. It
used to puzzle me at the time. It doesn't anymore. He was not fond
of his own black hair, which did not lie flat at the back, his sallow
complexion or his fused foot. He never looked at himself in a mirror.
He claimed he did not recognize himself.

Did I say already that his mother's name was Bia? And Bia
knew. Bia could probably smell me on his laundry.

Our rendezvous were brief and intense, wordless and increasingly frequent, and the fact that we were blatant infidels made it all
the more addictive. The mixture of his amorous embrace and the
chilly clasp of the evening audience intoxicated me until I believed
myself to be a moth emerging from my chrysalis. I had never been
held so tightly before and every time I surfaced from the pool or
from his arms, I felt as if I had found a place where I belonged.

It was illusory, of course, and it was only a matter of time
before it all had to end. I remember meeting Milo in secret one
night when I was desperate to hear him tell me once more that I was
beautiful. We sat in a service station cafe a few miles from the circus
camp, surrounded by half-eaten plates of cold chips and dirty cups
and saucers. I wanted to push my body across the laminated table
with the hard red plastic edges, scatter the plastic pots of tea and
little cartons of UHT milk and be as near to him as I possibly could
be. But the light was too bright and the sound of the traffic was too

loud. Instead I asked him if he took sugar in his tea, which was the next best thing under the circumstances.

"You don't know me, do you?" he said softly.

"I do," I replied.

"No," he said. "Where have I come from?"

I can't help blushing as I remember this conversation. I knew him intimately, the back of his neck, the dense texture of his hair, the mole on his left thigh, I knew him all over. But I didn't really know who he was. He was right.

"The same place as me," I replied. "From the circus."

"No," he said, "I mean originally. Everybody comes from somewhere."

"I love you," I said because although I didn't feel it, I was still waiting for it to happen automatically.

But he simply sighed and stared out of the window at the cars that streamed below us. And then he started to talk. I can't remember the exact words because many of them blew past me while I gazed at the reflected headlights that sped across his eyes. But I do remember that he said that love did not exist. He told me that along with faith and luck, love is a lie that makes life more bearable. He used the circus, his circus as an example.

"People want to escape the reality of their lives," he said. "They want to believe that they are special, that they will become the hero of their own destiny, if not today then maybe tomorrow. We exploit this. It makes them happy. It makes me money."

By the time he had finished, the tea was cold and undrinkable, the cold chips had been taken away and I knew that I had fallen without a net.

"You don't really believe that," I said.

"Yes I do," he replied. "I am a pragmatist."

"I see," I said finally, even though I didn't.

"Good," he said. "For many girls it is hard to understand."

I sat quite still, each breath a struggle as I tried to contain my tears.

"And what about Clara?" I said very quietly.

"Clara has her clothes. And I have her. We are not satisfied. We both live a lie but at least we know it."

That night, half the red neon heart on the top of the tent fused, leaving a curved tube, which looked like a hook.

Of course, Clara found out. How could she not? Valentine's was awash with spies and informers. And despite all that Milo had said, she still clung on tight to what she regarded as her property. But I wasn't in the least bit scared, not initially anyway. I was too upset for fear. Milo's words made me question everything. Suddenly the world was flat and old and used, not literally, but emotionally. If love is a lie to make life more bearable, then what is the point? I too had arrived at the conclusion that the public en-mass is lemming-like in their actions, but could the same be said for the individual? And if so, why did it hurt so much?

I became pensive and withdrawn; I lost my appetite and became as thin as a discarded candyfloss stick. Milo didn't seem to notice at first. And then when he did, claimed I kept poking him with my hips and jabbing him with my elbows. Finally I decided to reveal to him that our relationship was making me ill. He was silent for a moment and then produced a couple of vials of yellow and pink pills, which, he claimed, would make me feel better. When, after much persuasion, I swallowed one of each, he gave me the whole lot and told me to take some two three times a day.

This was a mistake. The pills were some kind of Benzodiazepenes—tranquillisers often prescribed to neurotics, schizophrenics, manic-depressives and suicidal people. I don't know where Milo had got them from, but they had the desired effect. Life sort of misted over, my problems receded and I drifted around feeling soporific. I felt as if I had just relaxed into a padded cell that was soft, warm and utterly safe. My sentences shrank to those of one or two words and when Milo came to my caravan at specially arranged times, I had usually forgotten and he would find me lying in my pyjamas counting the chewing gum balls that had been pinged at the ceiling. As for love, I didn't care about it anymore.

That was why I didn't see the signs. I didn't heed the danger

signals that were flashing, and clanking from every conceivable corner. A few of my old friends tried to warn me. They came to see me
on bogus errands but it was too risky to say out loud what everyone
already knew. And so they asked me how I was and then asked
me again, but I was completely oblivious and would always reply,
finethankyu and walk away.

As I said before, Clara knew and Clara would not tolerate it.
It strikes me now that it was strange that she didn't tackle her faith-
less husband. But she was of the school of women who saw female
as temptress and man as helpless victim and so it simply didn't occur
to her that it may have been easier for a man of 42 to seduce a virgin
of 16 rather than the other way around.

I remember that Milo was distinctly twitchy on the day that
it all came to a head. He looked at me deeply and then turned away,
like someone trying to memorise an object for future reference, or
like a contestant on a quiz show grappling with a question that
was too difficult and knowingly forsaking the star prize of a luxury
kitchen or a holiday for two in the Caribbean.

"Seeyu Thursday," I said softly.

"Of course," he said and then bowed, shut the door gently
and shuffled off round the back of the Helter Skelter. I remember
the beat of his stick as it ran along the wooden railings of the pony
enclosure, sounding as quick and regular as a racing pulse.

That night, wearing my blue dress and my pair of lamé wings,
I caught sight of Clara standing at the other side of the ring. She was
staring at me while her long nails were ripping long holes in a pair of
old nylon tights. I didn't think much of it at first. Her routine was
the first of the second act and she often watched the first half of the
show just to reinforce her own inherent sense of superiority.

As I climbed the rope to reach my paper horse, my mind was
still numbed, subdued and fixed on nothing in particular. The big
top was packed and the audience's breath rose up in pale curls. But
then I suddenly smelled the faint whiff of bear. My days at the circus
rewound until I heard a voice again, his voice, the bear man's voice,
not words exactly but the tone, the timbre. And then I noticed

something was wrong, something didn't feel right. It may have been the pinpoints of light in the orchestra's eyes or a peppery taste in the air, but suddenly I knew I had to pull myself back, to push and push from the depths of the pudding-like state I was in, and to surface in the present. Medically, this should have been impossible. I had taken enough sedatives to knock out a cow and could only focus for about ten feet in any direction. And it was hard to concentrate especially since everyone was watching and listening as I sang *You Only Live Twice* in my usual rather droll manner.

As the horse started to blaze around me and the drums began to roll, I came back to myself and instantly noticed that the level of water in my pool was far lower than it should have been. It was a few inches rather than several feet while the dark staining of the sand around its base indicated a serious leak.

I paused. The smell of paraffin and burning paper enveloped me. If I dived, I would die from horrific injuries. If I stayed where I was, I would perish from horrendous burns.

Right now, the very thought of my hopeless situation makes me feel utterly nauseous, but back then I suddenly remembered who I was, what I was capable of and what I wanted. And I came up with a solution, which to this day is still legendary among escapologists. They called it the Angel's Descent, because, right in front of hundreds of gullible children, cynical adults and murderous onlookers' eyes, I launched myself from the burning horse and slowly, very slowly, descended with no visible means of support down, down into the ring where I alighted on tiptoe with a slight and graceful flutter.

It was a stroke, I now see, of pure inspiration, the kind that only strikes you when the situation is truly desperate. Even the drummer stopped playing and watched my angelic journey from the high to low seemingly unsupported, and as I landed, the applause, when it came after an amazed pause, was deafening. I never told anyone how I had performed this trick and for years many thought I was either blessed, damned or both.

But, as I have already detailed, I was experienced in the art of illusion and there, high up in the big top, the idea came back to me like divine mental intervention. There was a mirror suspended from the roof. It was positioned to give the audience a bird's eye view of my death-defying plunge. I turned, and with one twist of the wrist, flicked it round to face a spotlight. In this brief illumination, the audience, momentarily blinded, didn't see me slip from my blazing platform and on to a rope that slanted down to the back of the tent. By the time the sunspots in their retinas had faded I had positioned two more mirrors and had created an apparition of myself as a floating spectre in the centre of the ring, while my real physical self carefully slid down the rope in the wings. The only part of my trick that was difficult was the last where I had to swap places with my mirrored image. Luckily, an opportune jolt in the power supply and a few seconds of darkness at exactly the right moment, left me free to complete the spectacle and take my bow.

It was a triumph, my dear. A real one-off. For several minutes I basked in the glory of my success. Three standing ovations, a bouquet of white carnations and blue lilies (which I suppose had been intended for Clara) and more cheers than anyone had ever heard before at Valentine's, all combined to show me what I needed to know; I didn't need Milo Valentine anymore.

Back in the dressing room I shared with the trapeze girls, there was a strange sense of lull. They rushed out when I entered, their false eyelashes held between their fingers like poisonous spiders. Once I was alone, I started shaking, my whole body quivering and rattling at the thought of how close I had been to my own death. In my mind a sequence of scenarios played out; Dolly throwing fresh sawdust over the blood which still beat under my skin regardless; my own body, laid out flat and blue and lifeless, and the vision of my parents standing over my coffin with their tear-splashed bibles held in front of them. It was delayed shock made far more severe, I expect, by the effects of Milo's drugs.

When I rose to throw on my dressing gown, I noticed that there was someone approaching the dressing room, not from the ring but from outside. I thought it was Milo at first, but as I listened, couldn't hear the hollow acoustic of his built-up shoe or the tap of his stick. Carefully, I slid behind the dressing table and, still acting purely on instinct, I hid. The intruder came slowly and deliberately up to the swathe of fabric which acted as a door. But nobody entered. My ears strained as I tried to work out where the person had gone, in or out, around or above, but beneath the noises of the interval, the murmur of laughter and the crying wails of children, it was impossible to tell.

As I stood, my breath held tight inside me, my heart beating so loud I was convinced it was audible, I made out three short, sharp ripping sounds coming from the corner where I usually sat. A loaded pause followed. Then someone crept into the room, sighed loudly and walked towards me. It was a woman. Panic seemed to gag me. I was sure then that I had been discovered, sure that I was about to be pulled out from my hiding place and murdered. Instead the woman stopped a few inches from my terrified body and started to murmur and make preening sounds. Of course it was Clara and I had momentarily forgotten that my hiding place was behind a mirror. After she had gone, leaving a few shiny hairs on the floor and a smear of lipstick on a tissue, I worked out that she had tried to stab me with something sharp through the canvas wall of the dressing room. Crude, I must say, but probably quite effective.

As proprietor, Milo watched the evening's performances from a seat in the orchestra balcony. I stood opposite and tried to catch his eye, for despite my change of heart, I was sure he would not want his newest star to die before he was able to capitalise fully. But he ignored my visual pleas and hissed requests. And when he finally looked up at me at the end of the show, he did so as if he had never seen me before in his life.

That night I discovered how vulnerable I had become. Milo refused to acknowledge me. The lock on my caravan door had been changed. My former friends were all sound asleep and clearly didn't hear my knocks at their caravan doors and even the animals that I went to for warmth and shelter seemed so jittery that I didn't dare enter their stalls.

It was Bia who found me shivering in the darkened big top, almost delirious with cold. I knew I had to leave Valentine's but I was not prepared, I was not ready. Without a sound, Bia handed me a hot, sweet cup of tea. I held it tight and breathed in its steam. Five tea-leaves floated on the top.

"Look," I said. "The great bear."

The thought of bears carried me back again to The Eiffel, to the night I had met the bear man, to the caress of fake fur on my cheek. I sighed and took a sip. The constellation dissipated.

Bia led me to an ancient wooden caravan that I hadn't noticed before and unlocked the door. Inside, the walls were stained with damp and mildew and a bed was half-collapsed at one side. But I was in no condition to mind and I let Bia take off my shoes and wrap me up in an old blanket, which smelt of Vick's Vapor Rub.

"Thank you," I said. "For... for this."

She only nodded. Bia was a strange old woman. I had never heard her say one word, not one and her wrinkled face looked almost Red Indian. But you could sometimes tell by her eyes what she was thinking. I wondered just where she and her son had come from: America, India, China, Mongolia or the plains of Southern Russia. And then Bia did the most surprising thing. She sat down beside me and started to sing 'Jesus, Clean my Soul' very softly. But it was not in Tartar or Mongolian or Sioux but broad Glaswegian.

"I was a vicar's daughter," she said when she had finished. "He formed this circus before I was born. Claimed that miracles could happen in the ring, which were impossible in church. One day he lay down with a lion and didn't get up again... The lion was shot, of course. My mother had to refund all the people he had converted... it ruined her life."

Bia pulled herself up and headed slowly for the door, muttering softly. I lay awake after she'd gone just listening, too frightened to drift off in case I would never wake up. But Valentine's had shut its brightly lit eyes for the night and when I, too, fell asleep, I dreamt not of lions but of bears, bears that sang in unknown languages.

The next morning I woke up with a start. Something was

wrong. First I suspected that one of my limbs had been chopped off. With great apprehension I checked my legs, arms, fingers and toes, but they were all still there. It was not my body, however, but my ears, which were missing something. Outside, apart from the sound of birds and the wind, there was complete silence. I climbed out of my makeshift bed and stepped towards the door. It was only when I opened it that I believed that what had happened the previous night had not been a dream. I stood at the door of a tumbledown caravan which stood in the corner of an empty field. Patches of flattened grass and the occasional pile of horse dung were all that was left of Valentine's. I had been left behind in a derelict caravan, a caravan that had never been part of the circus convoy, at least not the circus I worked for. In retrospect, I should have felt indebted to Milo's mother. Clara had the stamina of someone who can shop all day without fatigue, whereas I had quite random bursts of inspiration, intercut with youthful torpor. It may have simply been a matter of time before a few more stains appeared on my dark blue costume and I became one more girl who ran away with the circus and never returned home.

Talking of home, by some amazing coincidence, some truly incredible stroke of chance, I had arrived back at a field that bordered the village green of my childhood home. It took me a while, however, to notice it. I looked out at the site and saw only absence. Everything was gone; everything solid, the actual architecture of my life had been dismantled and taken away. All that was left was the suggestion, the after-image, the space.

I was devastated, furious, humiliated, upset. I stood at the door of the derelict caravan and sobbed. Then, with a blanket still wrapped over my blue outfit and my wings sagging and creased down my back, I paced a few feet forward then a few feet back again and again until my feet in blue ballet shoes became sodden through with dew.

I had nothing: no clothes, no money, no friends, no transport and I distinctly remember a craving for the pink and yellow pills that I kept in a box underneath the sink of my caravan. It may have been partly due to evil withdrawal symptoms but I had never felt so wretched in my life. The seductive sensation of the three ovations, the flowers and the adoration from the previous evening haunted me until I had invented a whole new scenario where the audience loved me, Milo loved me, even Clara was just playing games. Surely, I told my deluded self, the circus was my surrogate family; surely they would never deliberately abandon me in a field in the middle of nowhere and head on to an unknown destination without me. It must, I told myself, be a joke or at the very least, a horrible mistake.

A large explosion brought me back to my senses. I looked up and saw a familiar puff of smoke rising from the other side of a hill. I suddenly recognised where I was. I must have looked a strange sight, inconsolable one moment and euphoric the next.

I half-ran, half-jogged up the road to my old house. At the gates, I turned and watched the traffic of little cars and miniature buses rush like tiny electric toys along the main road beside the river Clyde. I suddenly missed my parents phenomenally. I saw us sitting at the table eating what was supposed to be macaroni cheese made with tomato ketchup instead of cheese, and then I missed the me I used to be quite profoundly. It's hard to explain exactly what I mean. I was the same person, I know, but I had seen and done things that made the eyes that looked back down the hill the eyes of another person entirely. I walked slower then, unsure of how I would greet my parents, dressed, as I was, in a ridiculous costume with nothing to show for my year's absence but an old blanket which smelled of Vick's Vapour Rub.

I needn't have been so concerned. When I slowly rounded the bend of the drive that led up to the vicarage, I came upon a sign

---

PROPERTY OF THE QUARRY.
KEEP OUT.

The house was locked up, and judging by the thick layer of quarry dust on the front doorstep, had been so for some time. It dawned on me that the explosion I had heard that morning was louder than I remembered and the hill was a little smaller. When I looked a little closer, I spotted a bulldozer engaged in clearing our side of the hill of bracken. The hill was slowly being flattened.

Some things should always be there. Parents and hills should not just disappear in puffs of smoke. It is unnatural.

I broke into my old house through the downstairs lavatory window. If it was a crime, I was in no mood to care. The furniture was gone, the books cleared and the rooms all empty but for the cobwebs which stretched across the light fittings and the mouse droppings that were scattered across the floors. All empty, that is, except for my room. I pushed open the door, and there it was exactly the same as it had been when I left, give or take some dust and an air of almost undetectable sadness. I went in, sat down on the bed, climbed in and stayed there, lying quite still, for the entire day. And then, just before the sunset, something caught my eye outside the window. One green apple was hanging from a branch of the apple tree. I leaned out, picked it, and ate it all this time, sour or not.

I would have liked you to have seen my old house. It was not a beautiful building, it did not have turrets or battlements or a glass conservatory and the garden was overgrown and tangled with weeds. But even now, I can feel the texture of grey granite under my fingernails and know its exact dimensions as I walk mentally around its walls, past the hole where I used to keep prized rocks, and below the jackdaws' nests. Although I am never sentimental about old buildings, because in general, they stand for a lot longer than we do, for some reason, I loved that house before I left it and even more when I returned.

I stayed for seven days and in that time tried on all my old clothes and packed the ones that could be adapted or worn in bed. Most of them were too small for me and so child-like in their style I wondered how my mother could have let her teenage daughter look like such a baby. After searching the whole house, I found a few tins stowed in the cellar, forgotten remnants of my father's short-lived plan for turning it into a religious retreat, and ate them one a day until they ran out. I also discovered some candles shoved deep at the back of a cupboard and a chocolate Easter egg under my bed, which a younger me had never found.

Absence is never a complete process. Because when people have gone, they do not disappear as if they had never existed. They are not wiped out forever, but like fireworks leave a smell of gunpowder and the almost tangible sensation of presence. My parents were not there anymore but they had left evidence behind, the grooves on the floor beneath their bed, the patches on the wall where pictures had hung and the smell of new bibles and clean dishtowels. I have never believed in ghosts, just in the calligraphy of atmospheres.

Of course, I tried to find out where they had gone. One day I walked down the hill to the houses of the three old ladies who I had once read to. But all were empty and all proclaimed that they too were the property of the quarry.

The same evening I found myself walking the length of the Old Mill Road, looking into the back windows of the houses on Heather Street the way I used to. I could have walked round to the front and knocked on doors until I came up with some information. But I doubted that my parents would have divulged anything to anyone. They always referred to the other villagers as a rabble of uneducated heathens.

I can't explain why, but it did cross my mind that many of them had seen my circus act and hadn't recognised me. Vanity, I suppose, and pride, two sins my father would have despised, prevented me from trying to find out the truth.

The next day, I realised I had been too careless with the burning of candles. I was woken up by men's voices followed by loud hammering. I crept down the stairs and into an unnatural darkness. It was daytime in my room and yet night below. The men were in the process of hammering large planks of wood across all the windows.

Crouching on the stairs I overheard them talking. My house, like the others on the hillside, was to be demolished. I suppose they didn't want to take any risks that tramps and squatters would take up residence and then sue them for vast sums of money in the event of injury by falling masonry or explosion. I have nothing against the building trade personally. Nevertheless it seemed quite insane to knock down perfectly decent houses so they could break up a hill for stone to build new ones. But at that time they were crazy about building high rises and shopping complexes and motorways. When you see one, try and see it as a composite part of a hillside above a river on which I used to play.

Anyway, after spending most of the day hiding in the would-be religious retreat in the cellar until they had gone, I realised that it was time to leave. I couldn't live in darkness without food for much longer.

When I woke the next day a pale blue glow filtered through the cracks in the wood nailed across my bedroom window. It was brighter than sunlight and threw wan shadows into my room. Although only November, there was a thick layer of fresh snow outside, softening all noise and covering the scarred hillside until it was as white as a new page.

I dressed quickly in several religious jumpers, a pair of Wellington boots, a pair of pyjama bottoms that passed for trousers and an old skiing anorak. With socks for gloves and a bag of fresh underwear in my hand, I kicked a plank of wood until it split and then I climbed down the apple tree. As I walked down the hill, it started to snow again. And when I looked back, the house was hidden behind a whirl of white and my footprints had disappeared completely.

It's cold here too. So cold that I wear three jumpers, three pairs of socks, two vests and a hat. But how I love the snow. How I love it so. It muffles, covers, and blurs the stupid world below. It makes everything new again. At least for a little while.

I have sniffed the grey stone outside on the balcony. It could be her hill. It was wet and had the smell of moss and blast, if you know what I mean. But also it just smelled of oldness and sadness and mould. My fingernails broke as I ran them across its surface. Some things should always be there, like parents and hills.

Julie suggested on the telephone this afternoon that I go and live with her and Graham. Just until I sort myself out. She also said that there was nothing wrong with my legs, nothing whatsoever, and if I just put my mind to it I could walk or run, do cartwheels, whatever. The doctors told her. The specialists confirmed it. I am not a cripple, not a real one anyway. I said nothing. I let the silence go on and on until she was begging me to say something, anything at all. And then she was crying, making these big gulping gollups and telling me that she and Graham can't have children of their own. I hung up before she'd finished the sentence. I know it was a mean thing to do. I tried to call her back but her line has been engaged for hours.

I make myself a cup of tea and eat a bar of chocolate piece after piece, mouthful by mouthful, until it's all gone, leaving my mouth all sticky and my chest feeling clogged. My time has split into two. One is made of walls and hours, the other words and pictures.

In your window you burn a blue lamp. It smudges through the condensation on the glass and makes the room unreadable. I wonder where you've come from. I wonder where you will go now.

Act II

Chapter five

A Fresh Start

O nce again, I climbed aboard the blue train with the
orange seats. Nothing had changed, not the intermittent screech of
brakes and the jolt of the doors or the smell of hot metal and old
chip papers. This time, it was I who was different.

I hadn't bought a ticket because I was completely penniless
and climbed off quickly one stop after the inspector had boarded.
As the train pulled away and trundled towards Queen Street, I very
nearly jumped back on a train heading the way I had just come,
which had just pulled in on the other side of the platform. But suddenly, I sensed a tickle at the bottom of my stomach. It was November. I was almost seventeen. It was very cold. As with much of my
life so far, I decided that I could not go back, only forward.

I was standing at a station called Hyndland in the West End
of Glasgow. Snow fell lightly and sprinkled the red sandstone tenement roofs with dustings of pale grey. I knew the area vaguely, as my
father had once been friends with a vicar called Father Barney who
lived in the vicinity. He had held regular hymn singing marathons
where each hymn sung was 2p for starving babies or something, and

he used to call on my father at short notice to 'make up numbers.' At some point they had had an argument about the virgin birth and had ceased all communication apart from sending each other Christmas cards with competitively holy quotes inside.

It was to his door that I went to first, not knowing what I was going to say and half-dreading his crushingly firm handshake. For some reason I thought that he might know an address for a hostel for destitute girls, suggest some charitable employment or at a stretch inform me of my parent's whereabouts. My options, you see, were not that abundant.

The houses in the area were built by the Edwardians and had corner turrets and carved brickwork. Inside, the buildings were split into huge flats with stained-glass front doors and oriole windows. Father Barney's flat, I remembered, smelt of furniture polish and paraffin heaters and looked over a large and well-clipped bowling green with a MEMBERS ONLY sign outside.

I climbed the tenement stairs, my fingers trailing over the dark green tiles that lined the walls and, with a mounting sense of trepidation, rang the bell. After an inordinately long pause, it was opened, not by Father Barney, but by a young man with a deep red spectacle line across the bridge of his nose. I explained my situation, a little too hastily I now realise, assuming that he was some sort of junior cleric. And then I listened in a trance-like state as he stuttered that he had bought the flat two years ago and had no idea who Father Barney was or where he had gone.

Stunned, I continued to stand on his doormat until he had no option but to invite me in for tea. In truth I couldn't face the thought of heading back out into snow, not then, anyway, not with an increasingly noticeable tummy rumble and stone cold feet.

The living room was practically bare. All traces of Father Barney-like clutter had gone. The new owner cleared a space on a newspaper-strewn orange box and, after searching out two mugs without dried-in fungus crusted to the bottom, he placed a pot of Earl Grey and a plate of extremely stale chocolate biscuits on top.

"So," he said as he dribbled tea into two mugs. "You a student too?"

"Not exactly," I said.

I swallowed back tears when I told him, selectively, what had happened to me and before I could stop him, Mortimer Montelimar, as his parents had sadistically named him, flung his arm rather clumsily around my shoulders and told me not to worry and to keep my chin up or some such thing. It came out later that I reminded him of his Swedish au pair who had run off with a pop band and ended up in Australia working in a topless bar. But right then, I didn't care whether his motives were honourable or not. I was lonely, hungry and had absolutely nowhere else to go. And so, the tea was drunk, the biscuits were eaten and in a matter of hours I found myself installed in Father Barney's old flat with a landlord who, by his own admission, didn't care if I paid him rent or not.

Mortimer was a medical student. His parents had bought him the property as some sort of investment. The idea was that he would rent out a couple of rooms to his friends to cover the cost of the mortgage and live there for as long as he needed to. But Mortimer was so utterly absent-minded and his parents so outrageously rich, that after two years, being a landlord was still an unfinished task on the list of Things to Do that he made every morning on the back of an old envelope. Until I appeared uninvited, four of the five bedrooms of the ample and high ceiling flat remained empty.

Everything about Mortimer's life was unfinished. The decoration in the living room had been attacked in a fit of enthusiasm and then abandoned, leaving piles of peeled-off wallpaper, old paint-splattered sheets and rock-hard paintbrushes to collect dust in corners. One wall had been painted, and I use the verb loosely, a violent shade of orange as evidence of intent. There was also half-eaten food in the fridge, which had grown blue and green fur, unpaid bills on the hall floor which threatened legal action, brand new plates, saucepans and even a TV still in their boxes on the hall floor.

But was I any better? Although now firmly in one place, the

ground still seemed to speed beneath me, making me unable to see more than a day ahead at a time and making my feet itch whenever I looked out along the Great Western Road.

The next day, after a quick scan over the small ads in the local free paper, I found a couple of part-time jobs. And after two interviews where I told my potential employer that I was newly arrived back from finishing school in Switzerland, I was soon working in a fruit shop on a Monday, Wednesday and Saturday and twice a week in the evening as a nude model in the art school.

When I came home, I would cook, clean, clear up and then listen to Mortimer talk for hours about the function of the spleen, the order of vertebrae or the neural system. At the weekend, we went to the supermarket together or for a walk in the park and Mortimer talked endlessly about the procedures of brain surgery or the pitfalls of explorative gynaecology.

I am certain that when he first set eyes upon me he saw a project, a challenge for which he had worked out a strategy, a procedure and a possible conclusion. He had diagnosed himself, noticed that he was lonely and hadn't even realised it. But although on a couple of occasions, as if a trigger from some formative experience had been pressed, Mortimer bought me flowers, we never woke up in each other's arms or promised life-long fidelity. I must admit that it did cross my mind once or twice that he was a man who I should consider. He was not ugly, not unpleasant, not aggressive, never mean and certainly not unintelligent. And although I doubted that he would ever graduate, he was rich and as he let slip one night, was lined up to inherit a large estate in Argyll. But I couldn't do it. Apart from the first day when I let him put his arm around me, if his hand ever brushed mine or his eyes lingered for too long in my direction, I would flinch, draw back, then go to my room and stay there until morning. And besides, my experience with Milo had made me wary.

I never spoke about Valentine's and left most of the details of my life poorly sketched. And Mortimer just didn't ask. When he enquired how my day had been, with the nonchalance of an expert, I told him about the success of pear crop or the Spanish tomato crash. But in his favour, I have to say that he could be sweet and listened with feigned interest despite the obvious mundanity of my life.

As I posed for hours at a time in front of a room full of scratching pencils, I felt as flat, self-conscious and two-dimensional as their sketches. And yet I forced myself into the narrow space I had fallen into, learning to cook from the Sunday supplements, ironing everything including the tea towels and buying my clothes in day-long spending sprees from high street fashion chains. In the early evenings when it grew dark before five, I felt the buttery glow of the lights of Heather Street and inhaled the smell of steaming kettle and towels drying on radiators. I was an outside girl on the inside. It felt very peculiar to be ordinary at last.

The days turned to months. Christmas sparkled briefly with a huge Christmas tree, bought half-price from the fruit shop, and some bashed decorations that Father Barney had left. One night when the snow furled so thick that you could see no further than a few feet and, completely against Mortimer's wishes, I climbed over the fence and on to the bowling green. While he fretted from the fence that someone would see us, that we would be arrested and charged with defacement of property and that he was definitely coming down with hypothermia, I built a huge snow magician with a wand made of a stalactite of pure ice.

Later that week, Mortimer went home to see his parents and I decided to decorate the living room. A few days later, my arms aching, my hair spotted with paint, I had finished. The walls were pale blue and the ceiling, indigo. As I gazed up, the colours became the blues of the sky on a summer evening, the kind of warm night where the glaze is infinite and the oncoming night surrounds like a tightness in the chest.

It was then that I realised that I couldn't pile potatoes or place mixed nuts in bags for much longer and I certainly could not sit still long enough to be anybody's muse. I quit both jobs on the same day in January, not that my employers seemed to mind. Dizzy was the adjective one used to describe me. Distracted, aloof, slow, he added.

Wriggler, the other claimed, twitchy, hyper, unable to concentrate, loafer, laugher, he embroidered.

That night I flambéed pork with prunes and made salad de fruit avec chocolate Chantilly. Mortimer ate the lot, as usual, without comment. As I listened to his lavish description of how bile is produced in the stomach, I realised that I would never belong there, I would never fit in. It was almost time to leave.

After my affair with Milo, I didn't believe in luck, fate or destiny. I just believed that certain circumstances make one more liable to seek out other options. I wasn't going to let my life deteriorate into a slow domestic drama. And if nothing good was going to come to me, I had to go out and look for it.

The next day I walked for miles across the city, up past the University and down through Partick and Dowanhill. Against the right angles of the buildings and the grinding textures of grey and black, I began to see the perfect circles the rain made in puddles and the way that fallen leaves iridess.

I saw the first paper flyer blowing along a gutter. Then I caught sight of another tied to a lamppost, a third was pasted in the window of a cake shop and a fourth plastered to a phone box. I picked up a leaflet in an Italian cafe where I stopped for a cup of tea and for the first time in weeks, felt a billow of something related to relief. A circus. It wasn't Valentine's, oh no. On the flyer was a picture of a man floating in mid-air and the word, *Believe* in handwritten gothic writing. Below that was an instruction. "Scratch here," it said. A short piece of text appeared. "Real Magic," it read. "URSA MAJOR. A circus beyond circuses."

Of course, on one hand I was extremely apprehensive about renewing any contact with my former profession. On the other hand, this outfit seemed completely different from the kind of circus I had known. According to the details printed at the bottom of the page, the first night of a week-long run was the very next evening. I decided that I would go and see, that was all, before I made any decision.

Mortimer and I arrived ten minutes early and sat in the

third row from the front of a circus ring, in a small, rather decrepit tent that had been pitched on a muddy corner of Glasgow Green. Candles lit up the interior and long, deep blue drapes lined the canvas walls. There was a strange smell, I remember thinking, not of animals or stale sawdust, but of damp, hot wax and some sort of incense.

Together we formed a sixth of the entire audience. Most of the other people there kept glancing at their watches. Collectively, they gave the impression that they were just passing and had popped in for a quick look. There was no ticket booth, tickets or attendants at the door and a sign hanging from a chandelier asked us to donate what we wanted at the end.

"What kind of a show is this anyway?" Mortimer asked too loudly. "There isn't even a popcorn stand? Where are the girls in the skimpy leotards? Why on earth have you brought me here?"

Sometimes people say or do something which makes you twist like a coin from heads to tails. I didn't answer. I suddenly wanted so much for it to be good.

The show started around fifteen minutes late, with the appearance of a rather befuddled ringmaster. He was old, so old that his face and hands looked pockmarked and concertinaed, like badly laid bitumen. Black lined his eyes, red was smeared in a crooked line along his narrow mouth and he wore a creased, rather greasy dinner jacket and a dusty, threadbare satin top hat. But when he spoke, all the reservations, which were gathering despite myself, disappeared. His voice rang out in round, deep, polished, Scottish syllables. It had the kind of tone that reverberates inside you, like standing on a bridge when a train crosses.

"Good evening," he said. "And welcome to Ursa Major. Tonight you will experience an evening's entertainment like no other. Tonight you will see real magic."

And then with a smile like a trill of a baby grand piano, he lit a large green flare, spun round three times and vanished. My eyes were still blazing orange with after-image as I stared at the spot where he had been. But unlike my trick at Valentine's, there were no carefully placed mirrors in the tent, no strings, no sudden cuts in power. "Hole in the floor," said Mortimer so loudly that the whole audience shifted in their seats. "Obvious, really."

The ringmaster appeared again in the row of seats right behind us. I hoped he hadn't heard.

"The Four Elements," he proclaimed. "Please put your hands together and welcome the Masters of Matter."

From each corner of the arena came a puff of smoke. The first to enter the ring was Mr Air. He was equally elderly but much fatter than the ringmaster. With a large red nose, real not applied, an off-white linen suit which strained at the buttons and a wig, dyed an unnatural shade of burgundy, he looked not only an unlikely performer but as if someone should offer him some sort of assistance to the nearest seat. While the ringmaster played an accordion, slowly and deliberately he tottered around the ring. He struck me, I am afraid to admit, as absolutely pathetic.

"Mr Air," the ringmaster continued. "Ever since ancient times, we have known about the four elements. Air, fire, earth and water. We are made up of all of them, air flows through our bodies, water is in our blood, earth runs through our bones and there is fire in our hearts. Close your eyes and press and you can see the flames that burn inside us all. And water, we are nothing if not water. Eighty percent, at the last count. Eighty percent. These elements hold us close to the earth, but we still have an affinity with the celestial. Who has not dreamt of flying? Now watch carefully to see a little light levitation."

Mr Air began to bounce up and down. He huffed and puffed and wheezed until I wondered if he was about to have a heart attack. And then, while continuing to bounce, he tied a piece of string to his huge waistband and handed the other end to a little girl in the front row. I glanced at Mortimer but he was leaning back in his seat with a sardonic expression on his face. A small gasp rose from the audience. When I looked back, Mr Air had risen a few inches from the ground and seemed to hang there for just a fraction of a second. With a small sigh, he came down again and then bounced higher and higher again until once again he looked as if he was hovering without any visible form of support near the roof of the tent. On the next occasion he looked quite suspended—he pulled out a banana, started to eat it and then motioned for the little girl to give the string a tug.

"Yes," the ringmaster boomed. "Mr Air has oxygen running through his body, wind in his very soul."

The little girl pulled. Mortimer guffawed. I frowned. Mr Air came down to earth a few milliseconds later with an audible thump and a flutter of his wig. He steadied himself before he bowed to a round of rather startled applause. And then, with the loping run of a large rhinoceros, he galloped off. It was much less impressive than my trick, the so-called Angel's Descent, but spectacular never the less.

"Trampoline beneath the sawdust" said Mortimer. "You can see the line. Look. Plus of course the optical illusion created by such a large mass in such a limited space."

Next came Mr Fire, an octogenarian with long white hair who closed his eyes, lit a candle, held it to his mouth and then breathed with a cool blue flame. He was followed by Mr Earth, an elderly acrobat who simply demonstrated the properties of gravity with a few painful-sounding somersaults. Finally Mr Water climbed into a glass tank and revealed how he could breath underwater.

"Air tube up the sleeve," said Mortimer.

"You see, Ladies and Gentlemen," the ringmaster said to nobody in particular. "The human body is made of matter—magical, beautiful, changeable matter. Just remember the simple rule: Don't try any of this at home. At least not when anyone's looking."

"What a load of poppycock," said Mortimer loudly.

I wished at that instant that he would leave. But instead, Mortimer gave me an expansive commentary on how impossible in reality each particular trick was, using medical examples as proof.

"Where have they been for the last three hundred years?" said Mortimer.

A brief pause followed while someone in the wings coughed.

And then the ringmaster, who by now was sitting above us all on the lip of a chandelier clutching an accordion, introduced the next act, Ursa Minor, the Little Bear.

"At last," muttered my cynical companion. "A few mangy animals followed by a couple of crappy clowns. This is more like it."

The music started and I suddenly felt my spirits lift. There was a familiarity about the whole scenario, something I knew I'd seen before, I just couldn't remember where. A bear waltzed into the ring, not a real bear but a man in a bear suit. His fur glossed in the candlelight, his eyes crackled green and from a metal collar around his neck hung a long chain.

"Oh no," said Mortimer. "It's a man in a suit. This is interminably dull."

"Shut up," I hissed. "Just shut up."

The bear man danced slowly and despite his bulk and texture, with incredible grace. His movements were both comical and heart breaking and suggested fairy tales in cold places. At one point he threw a handful of water into the air and it fell as snow, real snow. A flake landed on my tongue and I tasted it. It was the strangest and most beautiful trick I had ever seen and to this day I have no idea how he did it. I felt myself lift from my seat, catch fire, spin in mid-air and breathe without oxygen. Metaphorically, I mean. Quite accidentally I had found the bear man again.

"I need a drink," said Mortimer when the first act had finished. "Coming?" When he looked at me briefly for confirmation, I shook my head. I knew I would leave him.

As I type, the silence all around seems to soak up my words. It is night and there are no stars, at least none that I can see. I am tired now; tired of typing, tired of running through the past like a road through a landscape where I know I can't stop.

My little Wing, today I wrapped you in a blanket and carried you down to the sea. It was St Andrews, I think. The wind was strong and we had to lean into it, like birds do. Out there, on the mottled surface, a couple of boats bobbed up and down. We were warm, you and I. People smiled at us, at our red cheeks and the way you laughed at seagulls. Now when you dream I can see your mind's eye looking up at the scratched blue sky and watching the constantly amazing waves. And I wish that I could see the world so utterly fresh again.

Ursa Major was closed down by the Department of Health and Safety the very next day. An inspector had been sitting in the audience disguised as a pensioner and reported them as a fire hazard and a danger to the public. It wasn't just the candles and the lack of facilities such as toilets and baby changing rooms, it was also the fact that the second act included an ancient female magician whose ten white rabbits escaped from her hat and were found consuming a child's school blazer, plus the re-appearance of the bear man as Mr Essence, and his free distribution to all of a health mixture which was found to contain alcohol.

Later, as I watched the bear man pace around the ring wearing an old-fashioned tweed jacket and a pair of ancient corduroys, I barely heard the words he was saying. Out of costume, I saw that his hair had been cut in a line level with his jaw but was so tangled and full of static that he looked a little like an electrocuted Elizabethan. But he was the same man, the same grisly who had escorted me to Queen Street Station many months before.

Sometimes, even now, his vaguely foreign drawl returns as if I have taped it in my head, and I recall snatches of his alphabet, the cures for aches, broken bones, coughs and drunkenness, eye-bulge and fatty thighs and giddiness and gout, heart disease, inflammation of the joints, jaundice, kleptomania madness, nicotine addiction, old age, phlegm, quick temper, rubella, sun-burn, toothache, vertigo, wounds and eczema—he couldn't spell. But then, right there, in the frayed tent on Glasgow Green, as his voice ran through me like oil on a rusty chain; something within came loose, unstuck. The bear man, as I knew him then, assembled a large long wooden trestle table covered in scorches and lit two small fires in bowls at either end. From a blue metal workbox, he produced a selection of powders in test tubes plus a veritable cocktail cabinet of liquids.

"First I warm up," he said. And like a conjuror of strange

substances, he started to juggle badly and fling… green powder mixed with red liquid made a small flash of light, purple grains sprinkled on a naked flame created orange puffs of smoke and when he emptied a vial of violet liquid, there were dozens of tiny explosions as each drop hit the ground. The children in the audience squealed with delight. Nobody in that tent had ever seen anything like it. Not even me.

Despite dropping several bottles and spilling a jar of what looked like salt all over the ground, the bear man had a sort of fumbling showmanship, a careless grace. He bowed at the merest suggestion of applause and blushed a deep scarlet whenever a trick failed.

"Oh deary me," he said out loud when the sleeve of his tweed jacket caught fire and he had to douse the flaming hem with a large glass of water he had been drinking from. Then, as the sharp, sour smell of burning wool filled the air, the bear man paused.

"And now," he said to no one in particular. "You are about to witness some herbal magic, some natural alchemy plus a couple of botanical miracles."

During the next fifteen minutes, he did the most amazing things with plants, roots, metals and herbs. Using a big old book, he followed what looked like recipes mixing petals with honey or ground garlic roots with goat's milk and iron fillings. The whole tent gradually filled with unusual smells and delicious scents as he created a tonic for baldness for a man in the second row and an aphrodisiac for an old woman in a mackintosh.

I felt quite elated. It wasn't just the demonstrations with Bunsen burners and tiny copper pestle and mortars but his vivid descriptions of the special secret properties of plants, flowers and metals.

"Saffron cures low spirits," the bear man said with a flourish. "Take too much and you'll laugh yourself to death. The Violet was called Nigra Viola in Latin and Ion in Greek. To relieve inflammation of the heart, or take away thirst, try using its beautiful sweet petals. Here, feel."

The texture of a violet petal on my cheek was like the warm stroke of a wood fire or the touch of a tentative lip. The flower was passed round until it became quite wilted. The audience tasted and sipped, laughed and frowned, sniffed and listened. This was a different kind of performance, like a cookery demonstration, a conjuring act and chemistry lesson all rolled into one.

Eventually I caught the bear man's eye over a bunch of mountain cowslips, or bear's ears, as he talked about stewed roots as a cure for vertigo. When he saw me, he jumped, visibly, in surprise. And without a doubt the strangest sensation rushed from my eyes to my heart to my belly. It was as if we were linked by a long golden rope, him at one side and me at the other. It was a tug inside, a ringing, singing shudder. The rescuer of dancing bears and sorcerer of plants was called Constantin. I can write no more tonight. His name scores all other words right out of me.

My eyes slide off the printed page. I listen to the quiet of my world. Rooooroooya, the shipyard siren, a wordless lament as the spectres of a thousand shipbuilders who make their way home from work. Rooooroooya.

Meeeeeefow; the thin streak of car brakes on the concrete of the motorway. Meeeeffff.

Waaawaaa; the hollow round bark of a tied up dog faced with a stranger in a black coat. Wu.

And then nothing. Nothing but the faint wail of the wind trapped in small places and the tiny creak of audibly shifting seconds.

The phone rings—prill, prill, prill prill. Double glazing salesman. Are windows durable, I ask? Do they withstand demolition?

The phone rings again. Julie. Can she come round now? She's in the area actually and she has bought a chocolate cake and no, Graham is not there too. I pull myself back down to the low horizons of my soon to tumble down world and wait once more for Julie.

The cake has Smarties all over the top and is homemade even though Julie claims she bought it from the bakers. I pick off the orange ones when she isn't looking. Today Julie is wearing her green outfit, her green dungarees, green socks and pale green cardigan. On her head she wears a yellow hat. She looks like the kind of ice-lolly that is always left at the bottom of the freezer in shops. The kind that stains your tongue.

"Have you thought any more about what I suggested?" she asks.

"What was that?" I say.

"You know," she replies. "About you coming to live with us for a while. Just until you get on your feet again."

I watch the spread of horror creep across her face as she realises what she has just said, then I sigh loudly and start to fiddle with my hair.

"Sorry. Shall I put the kettle on?" she asks when the pause stretches for too long.

"No," I say. "I can manage. I always have, haven't I?"

I throw up my arms and pull myself up on to my rings. Slowly, so slowly, I stretch out until I am almost hovering like a bee and stay that way, quite suspended, for a minute. Julie doesn't know whether to give me a round of applause or just pretend that nothing's happened.

"Sugar?" I ask, when I know she can stand it no longer.

"Two please," she answers.

Of course I don't stay on the rings, I just want to spin, leap and swing to show her what I can do. I boil the kettle, make a pot of tea and send it speeding back on a trolley into the living room. Julie is reading. She looks up at me with that expression she always uses when upset. First I think she has found my mother's manuscript, that she has been reading my inheritance, my only valuable thing in the world. I scream. I fly towards her from ring to ring, bullet-aimed with nails and teeth. But in the fraction of a second before I reach her, I see little coloured clusters of photographs. In her hands is my scrapbook of whacko, ads—my lonely hearts.

"Aaagh," she cries when she sees me coming, and drops the book on the floor. I land with a thump beside her on the sofa. Photographs and hand-written letters cover the carpet, hundreds of them forming a layer of paper and pictures.

"Julie," I say. "You shouldn't have. That's personal."

"Who are all these men?" she cries. "What have you become? Some sort of Jezebel?"

I start laughing. I can't help it. I laugh and laugh until my side aches. Julie is staring at me like she's decided I am someone unfathomable, someone who does unsavoury things that she doesn't understand. Her eyes flit around the flat, looking for signs, I suppose, for the odd sock or the extra toothbrush.

"Read them," I say. "Go on. Try this one. It's from Josh."

Cautiously, Julie lifts up the letter, holding it by its very outer edges.

"Dear Jin," she reads.

"An original start," I say and start to pour a long amber stream of tea into two mugs and cut myself a large slice of cake.

"Thank you for your letter," Julie continues. "How fascinating to have travelled the world as a tightrope walker... Niagara falls must have been particularly problematic."

She reads the rest in silence, her eyes flitting back and forth across the page like an executive toy.

"He sounds very nice," she concludes.

"No he doesn't," I retort.

By this time, I am back in full swing, so to speak, my mouth full of cake and my head quite high with all that sugar and cocoa.

"Is that the one who spelt angst with an x?"

"You can never tell," Julie continues, "from a letter. I met Graham..."

"He's a moron," my voice overlaps. "A half-wit, a buffoon, they all are. Why else do you think they'd be desperate enough to reply to a..."

"Through a personal ad," concludes Julie.

"...personal ad" I say.

We look at each other in silence. Like a farce or a sitcom comedy. Julie isn't laughing. Neither am I.

"It figures," I say eventually. "Graham. They're all Grahams. Couldn't you have given him a road test before you got married?

That's the trouble with mail order. Don't know what you're getting."

Julie stands up. A photo booth shot of a boy called Clement drops from her lap and falls over and over, white paper, big smile and curly hair, white paper, big smile and curly hair.

He looks quite nice upside down.

"I think I better go," says Julie.

"But you haven't had any cake," I say. "Or tea."

"No," she says. "I've changed my mind. We can't continue like this. It's hopeless, hurtful, unconstructive… I wish you'd bloody grow up."

"What? Are you allowed to say that?"

She swallows but doesn't look at me. I can tell she thinks she never wants to see me again. Heads and tails, she suddenly despises me.

"Julie," I say. "Julie?"

"Goodbye," she says.

The door closes gently behind her and I count her footsteps on the stairs until they fade away. One hundred and seventy four.

"Julie, you silly old biddy!" I hear my own voice shouting. "Come back. I was only joking."

The cake changes as the light fades. First it's glossy and slightly greasy and then it begins to get all crusty. The Smarties seem to sink into the icing one by one. The spaces where the orange ones were look like moon craters. I think about Mortimer. It's not nice to be the one who gets left behind. I hang from my rings and spin and spin, round and round, faster and faster until my ropes are as tightly wound together as I feel inside.

Outside I can hear the crash and wallop of furniture being moved. The light is fading and in your block, more windows are now black, more and more houses are empty, more hopeless cases lifted and shifted somewhere else. But still your light turns on every evening. We are like two lighthouses, you and I, two people turning and turning but going nowhere, blipping and flashing in the still, cold night.

Chapter six

The Chemical Marriage

Some people feel compelled to hoard insignificant items like bus tickets and Christmas cards and unusual pebbles from beaches. They can recite dates and places and even what they ate for breakfast ten years ago with ease. I never kept anything. I threw everything away. Letters, bills and even cheques, which nestled between the pages of newspapers, were binned, accidentally of course, when the pile became too big. Telephone numbers, receipts and green paper dry-cleaning tabs were washed, dried, and became the balls of pulp in the bottom of pockets. Even photographs seemed to evaporate from their place in my album, leaving only empty spaces and a few splatterings of dried-up glue.

Now I wish I'd kept them all more carefully. My memories, I suppose are random, my narrative is quite objective. A story can be told a million different ways depending on who's telling it.

What will you remember of me, my little one? A certain scent of milk and skin and my long pale hair.

It's daytime again and the sun streams through the windows of my caravan and soaks up night, the doubt, the irrational fear of the unknown. Even the corners look safe. What I remember of Constantin was his thick dark hair, the way it curled on the back of his neck as if it wanted to be as close to the special, secret softness of his skin as I did. And the way it trapped the light and held it for hours after, like rock warmed by sunshine.

I remember that it was raining that night on Glasgow Green, the endless drizzle known in Scotland as smirr. I was just seventeen and dressed all in red. It was the fashion then—one colour—dress, tights, shoes, coat and lipstick, a sort of all over shade. If I stood against a post-box I was practically invisible. It was dark, cold and wet and pools of water had collected on the makeshift wooden floor of the tent. At the end of the performance I sat and watched the meagre audience gather their things together and start to leave, a few of them placing their spare change in the hat the ringmaster had left in the centre of the ring. In my hand was one of the little bottles Constantin had distributed. "Elixir of health," was written in biro in an unsteady hand. It smelled strongly of rum and so I drank it.

The bear man didn't see me when he came back to count the takings in the hat. He knelt down and coin by coin made lots of little piles of coppers and silver on the sawdust.

"Five pounds and sixty three pence," he shouted out loud eventually to nobody in particular. "Not a fortune but it is a beginning."

I rose from my seat and silently approached him. I had no idea what I was going to say or how I was going to say it. In fact my knees shook so violently I thought I might fall over.

"Excuse me," I said after standing behind him for a minute just waiting for him to notice me. "Excuse me. Can I audition?"

He turned, stood up and jumped all at the same time, making his body sort of half-leap, half-squirm away from me. After a long hard stare, he spoke.

"What?" he said.

"I am a performer," I said. "Currently on the look-out for new opportunities."

He coloured and nodded slowly.

"Sorry," he said while continuing to nod. "No vacancies."

We both knew that we had met before. I knew that he was a bear stealer. He recognised me as an underage drunk, but still we kept up the pretence of formality. It was a kind of game, a childish charade, a subtle seduction.

"But surely," I replied. "You would like to see what I could do? Your circus is rather intriguing and yet it lacks a certain… something."

"I know," he said, still nodding. "I like it this way. What do you do, just as a matter of interest?"

In the corner of the ring stood the tank, which Mr Water had used in his act. Up above there were no platforms or high wires, just a long rope dangling from the centre of the tent. But there was also a paper moon hanging from a couple of wires which the lady magician had used in a rather poor trick which demonstrated some principle or other using a couple of forks stuck into a cork and placed in the mouth of a milk bottle.

"I jump," I replied. "I jump into a tank of water from a burning horse. Watch."

I was vaguely aware of his protests but ignored them. I pulled off my coat, shimmied up the rope, positioned the moon above the tank, set fire to it rather presumptuously and jumped.

At least that's what I might have done but when I woke up, my memory of those entire few minutes had been wiped out. I would have liked to have told you that I came round in a nice soft bed saying, "Where am I?" or at least in his arms in a Pieta-like pose. But instead the first thing I knew was blackness and violent pain. And when I tried to open my mouth to scream, I deduced with a wince that I had landed face down in the sawdust.

What happened was that the heels of my shoes had become entangled in the rope and I had fallen off the burning moon. It was not the dignified descent I had intended but a fully-fledged belly flop on to the hard, cold ground. Mortimer was wrong, I vividly remember thinking as I lay there, spitting globs of pink dust. There was no trampoline, no softly cushioned bounce to break my fall.

"Oh my God," said a voice up above me. "Stop. Look at me. Smile?"

"What?" I stuttered.

"No it's okay, I can see," came the reply. "You haven't lost any teeth. This is good."

In my handbag, I carried a small powder compact. I sat up, pulled it out and examined my face. Purple bruises were appearing down one cheek. The other was grazed with large scrapes of dark crimson blood. I had also bashed my knees, twisted an ankle and had ripped large holes in my clothes. As I realised that my outlook was certainly not good, I remember his mumbled words.

"Everything else can be just about fixed. But teeth. No way. You need to mix mercury with mistletoe and apart from the poisonous side effects; they often make the whole set go black. No, just as well there was no tooth loss. Well… thank you for showing me. I think you need to work on a less dangerous act."

I was stunned. He couldn't really have thought that my fall was intentional, could he?

"That wasn't it," I said. "I mean, I fell."

"I saw that," he said and he smiled, his mouth drawn with the same flamboyance I had noticed before.

"Don't," I said. "It really isn't funny."

"I'm sorry. I'll walk with you to the train station," he said.

I stood up, shakily and took a tentative step. Shooting pains shot up my leg.

"Any brandy?" I asked. "Whisky? You know, something medicinal?"

He eyes ticked and I saw him picturing me the last time we met.

"I don't think that's a good idea," he said.

"I suppose," I said a little too loudly, "that this means that I don't get the job."

As I struggled with tears, his mouth pursed. Then it burst out, a gurgle of hilarity, an explosion of mirth.

"You are a strange girl," he said eventually by way of explanation.

And so there we were, him laughing and me crying, hot and cold, dry and wet, happy and sad, although I now know, which was which was not as clear cut as it then appeared.

After that we introduced ourselves, formally, tentatively, soberly as he bandaged up my cuts and bruises. I repeated his name over and over in my head, rolling over the unfamiliar phonetics with the tip of my tongue. Constantin, Constantin, Constantin.

It was late by then, after midnight at least. And so he agreed that I should stay for one night if only for the sake of observation. After I had convinced him that there was no one I should phone and after he had blown out all the candles and pocketed the takings, he accompanied me to his caravan.

Reading this over now it does sound a little suspect. Should a young, vulnerable girl have willingly accompanied a man whom she hardly knew to his sleeping quarters? But at the time I thought myself neither vulnerable nor particularly young. And, as I am sure you will have gathered, I felt I knew him, I trusted him. In fact it was I who hesitatingly suggested it, after he had mused for at least five minutes over where I should sleep.

"If you don't mind," he said.

"Really, I would be extremely grateful," I replied.

Even in the near dark, Ursa Major hid its magic well. The trailers and caravans were made of wood, their doorways, windows and spooked wheels carved with elaborate scrolls and painted in what were now faded colours. It was all very charming, but slightly dilapidated and there was a vague smell of mothballs and stewed tea.

Constantin's caravan, however, was different. It was modern with rounded corners and shiny chrome edging. Inside there was the smell of Tupperware and old picnics. Everything was orange, the curtains, the seat covers, and even the handles on the cupboards. He had just bought it, he told me, second hand.

"It used to belong to a Mr and Mrs Tangerine," he said. "They had an orange cat too."

I don't know why that was funny, even now. But both of us laughed. I think he made it up, actually, but that was what he was like. He had a ridiculous sense of humour.

It must be said that the caravan was not ideal for a man of his size. Once inside, he had to stoop and he was forever banging his head, shins and elbows on cupboards, draining boards and fold-able tables. I climbed into a sleeping bag on Constantin's bed while he collected up some cushions and laid them in a line on the floor. Neither the floor nor the bed was long enough for him to stretch out and it was clear he would have to almost double up.

"Are you sure this is okay?" I asked several times. But he said he would not have it any other way.

Before we struggled with our clothes under the covers with the light off, he offered me something to make me sleep. And as he sat down on the bed beside me, I felt his breath on my neck, his closeness, and the slight tremor of his hand. He poured oil of lavender and some juice of boiled poppy leaves into an orange plastic spoon. He swallowed. I opened my mouth. He pushed the spoon inside. I held it between my teeth. I swallowed. When he pulled it out, there was a small curve of tooth dents in the plastic. Then he did something very strange. He took my hand in his, turned it over, held it to his face and inhaled long and slow. When he let it go again, there was a perfect purple circle an inch below the knuckle.

"Sleep good," he said.

Then I slept, not like a baby as babies sleep in fits and starts and wake at all ungodly hours, but more soundly and deeply than I had for months. I woke at eight A.M., by the light of his luminous clock, and lay awake just listening to the regular wash of his breathing. It was good to be within thin, flimsy walls of metal again, to lie in the pale orange light and to be a few steps away from fresh green grass. I closed my eyes and imagined the tarmac race underneath my wheels once more.

But as I have described, Ursa Major was not an ordinary

circus and it was nothing like Valentine's. There were no half-dead goldfish or spangled trapezists. And it wasn't about trickery or extortion but something all together more bizarre. Although right then, I wasn't sure exactly what that was.

In the citrus coloured light, Constantin's face was quite still. His hair fell around his face in loose curls and his unshaven skin was pale blue. As I watched him sleep, I remember wondering what he had done with the bear. And then, with a loud sigh, he woke up.

"Breakfast," he said, as he sat bolt upright and threw his arms out in a long cat-like stretch. "Yes, I think so. I go for a walk first. I'll be back soon."

He told me that whenever he was in a new place, he went out walking. He would stroll into neighbourhoods and observe, listening to the pounding of music from open windows and the sound of children crying on doorsteps, noticing mown lawns or peeling paint work and sniffing out each faint whiff of illness, damp or perfume.

"I like to think I can smell the nature of places," he said.

That morning, when he came back with a couple of doughnuts in a bag for me, there was a circle of yellow tape right round the whole circus encampment. A sign had been hung which read,

---

NO UNAUTHORISED PERSONNEL

---

and a man in a mustard-coloured car coat with a clipboard shifted from foot to foot at the main entrance. I had watched him tape up the circus from the window of the caravan earlier. He had had some difficulty and at one point had chased the yellow tail of tape halfway across the park.

The man explained the situation to Constantin who simply nodded. He didn't return to the caravan but disappeared into the maze of the encampment. Ten minutes later, I noticed a trail of elderly circus performers head towards the big tent. They were all bleary with sleep and a wig-less Mr Air was still wearing his striped pyjamas. He didn't seem quite so bouncy now.

I wondered what I should do next. It seemed inappropriate

somehow to lie in bed, so I decided to get dressed. Although they had healed, dare I say miraculously, my bruises made me stiff and it took considerably longer than usual. By the time I arrived in the big tent all but Constantin and the Ringmaster, whose name was Magnus, had left.

"We have no choice, Magnus, but to pack up and leave today," Constantin was saying. "It's an official something or other. An order thing. If we stay, I am told we are liable to huge fines and maybe a jail sentence. It is quite meaningless to stay."

As if they heard my almost silent breathing instantaneously, they both turned.

"Aah, there you are," said Constantin. "Jam or sugar."

He held up a paper bag where a pair of doughnuts rustled.

"What you need, if you don't mind me saying," I said after a short pause, "is me. I know all about rules and regulations. I know all about government acts and publicity and stuff."

Magnus turned to Constantin enquiringly, but Constantin simply raised his hand. He was blushing again.

"This is Helena…" he said.

"You're quite good," I interrupted. "But too old… um fashioned."

The ringmaster frowned.

"People want thrills," I continued quickly. "Danger, nerve, dexterity. And what's more, they enjoy it a great deal more if they have to pay for it. If you came up with an offer I'm sure we could come to some arrangement."

And then I tried to smile a Valentine smile only my face wouldn't comply. They paused for an instant and both stared at the floor. And in that fraction of a time, that fate-making space, I suddenly felt a rare sensation that placed me there, in that exact present, and cleared my mind of everything else. Is this what I really want? I asked myself.

But I knew that I would have done anything to be part of Ursa Major, to perform in the old blue tent to the music of chinkling chandeliers and wheezy accordion, where the air was filled with strange smells and blue burning flames. More than anything else, I wanted to be with Constantin, the bear man.

Magnus shook his head.

"I'm sorry," said Constantin. "But as I told you. It's impossible. This tour is over. I'm sure you'll find other employment very soon."

I looked at him, at the wilted paper bag of doughnuts in his fist, the ruffle of sleep in his hair and the shrug of concern in his face. But he did not look back.

"Good luck," said Magnus, his big voice filling every inch of the silence. "And Constantin and I thank-you for your kind offer."

I turned and limped away from the tent, away from Ursa Major and away from the life and the man that I wanted so badly. Out in Glasgow Green I walked around the fountain, through the large archway at the entrance and down towards the Clyde. Everything hurt again. Everything ached. I stared at the grey water of the river as it flowed by, aware that it was going somewhere, whereas I was stuck. I was pathetic, defeated, injured.

"Self-pity is self-indulgence," I suddenly said out loud. "I must not give up so easily."

They had packed up the big blue tent by the time I returned, bag in hand and wearing a change of clothes. Mortimer had been up all night, studying for an exam. When I told him that I had met some friends on my way home, had tripped coming down some stairs in a pub and had to spend the night in Accident and Emergency, he believed me. Even though I had no friends. Even though I had never set foot in a pub in all the time we had known each other. He looked me over, inspected the bandaging and the bruising, paused briefly at the eclipsed full moon on my hand, and recommended Paracetamol.

"I've been thinking," he said as he whisked off his spectacles and started to polish them on an edge of curtain. "Why don't we go out some time? On a date?"

"No, thank-you," I said. "But it is sweet of you to offer."

"Oh well," he said as he put back his spectacles. "Worth a try."

I left him a note pasted to the television where I knew he would find it. I also filled the fridge with expensive ready-made meals and left a neatly ironed pile of clothes on his bedside table. I was sure he wouldn't miss me for at least a fortnight.

A circle of cars, caravans and large trailers stood in the yellow-taped off part of the park. Everything else had been packed away. Constantin stood eating a doughnut beside a moss green car, to which his caravan was hitched. As for me, it was not difficult to remain unseen. There was a huge crowd of people at the yellow perimeter held back by a single policeman. Magnus, the Ringmaster, was talking to a man at the front. Whoever he was, he had a new growth of thick black hair on his head, which he continually fingered.

"I used to be a red-head," I heard him say loudly.

It was then I noticed a convex mirror nailed to a tree for the use of vehicles pulling out of the park and into the sharp bend of the main road. There was another mirror in a children's playground a few hundred yards away. In retrospect it was a dubious set up, a high-risk trick as there were a multitude of factors that could interfere and spoil the effect. When I had surreptitiously positioned the mirrors exactly, I was far more nervous than I had been sitting on a burning paper horse thirty feet above the ground. I was so scared that I felt dizzy. I had only one chance. But it was this, I told myself, or the cold grey waters of the River Clyde.

Carefully, I climbed up a large beech tree into the beam of both mirrors. And then, almost confident that I was more or less invisible, I slipped painfully down a rope and on to a patch of grass directly behind Constantin's caravan. The door was locked. I twisted and turned the doorknob in both directions and even gave the door a small shoulder shove but it did not fly open like doors do in films. And then I heard the sound of someone coming. My trick worked so long I was in an exact locality. But I wasn't. I turned and dived back to the trampled spot beneath the tree and swayed, toppled and steadied myself as I lost my balance and then regained it. What Constantin saw, he told me later, was the strangest sight, a blue girl disappearing and reappearing again, each time surrounded by a prism of light.

He said he thought he was hallucinating. He blamed a new concoction he was experimenting with, made of sealing wax and crushed millipedes. What he really thought, I'm still not altogether too sure. I like to think he knew it was me all along. Anyway, he unlocked the caravan, fetched a book from inside and then climbed into the driver's seat of his car.

I made a dash from my invisible spot to the door once more and jumped inside the caravan just as the convoy started up its engines and began to snake in slow single file out of the Green. Although there was almost a minor traffic accident involving a hearse due to my re-positioning of the mirror on the tree, the circus moved on while a crowd of disappointed spectators, still held back by the tireless policeman, looked on.

You may think that after the first time, I should have known better than to stow away in a caravan on the move. But that is exactly what I did. Circumstance, I had decided, would not dictate my life. I had been through too much to spend the next sixty years wondering when I might happen to meet Constantin again by accident. I would act first and deal with the consequences later, for, as you may have realised, I am not and never have been a coward.

As we slowly drove out of the city, I felt a little sickened by all the jolting. At the back of a small cupboard underneath the sink, I found a bottle of infusion of clove flowers for the cure of dizziness, which was fairly close, I judged, to car-sickness. It tasted quite pleasant so I drank almost half of it and then promptly fell asleep on Constantin's bed.

When I woke up, the caravan was slowing down. It was early evening and a strange dappled light reflected across the ceiling. Through the window I saw a huge snow-covered mountain and a wide expanse of water. A light mist was unrolling above the surface and a few birds left long ripples with the tips of their wings. We had come north, north to the deserted valleys, high desolate peaks and deep lochs of the photographs on a calendar my mother used to hang in the kitchen. Suddenly the wheels of the caravan bounced off the tarmac of the road and on to the grass verge before lurching to a halt. We had arrived somewhere or other at last.

I listened to the murmur of voices as the circus troop slowly climbed out of their cars, stretched their arms and stamped their feet in the cold, clean air. I tried not to worry about what would happen next. Would I be discovered and banished or discovered and welcomed? Wherever we were, it wouldn't be as easy just to send me away with a no thank-you. The least they would feel obliged to do, I reasoned, was to offer me some food, for after bypassing the doughnut for breakfast, I was starving.

But Ursa Major, the circus, had reached its destination, while the circus performers had not. My ears strained as their voices started to fade. And then I made out a scraping sound followed by vague splashing. Finally, when I was certain that they had gone, I opened the caravan door. Out on the water, a rowing boat was heading to a large island on what was a small inlet of the Atlantic sea.

Later, I sat on the lip of coast and watched the lights come on in a house on the other side of the sound. A flicker in a downstairs window suggested a roaring fire and I even imagined I caught the smell of roasting chicken. In the water beside me, a seal popped up its puppy-like head and observed me for a few minutes. It looked a little like Mortimer so I was quite glad when it ducked down and swam away. There was nothing else on either side of the coast but the house, no villages, no street lights, no train tracks, nothing, just steep wall like-rocks jutting straight down into the fathomless sea. It was too dark to look for another boat and so I resigned myself to another night in the caravan. They would come back, I was certain, the next day. And then I would present my services once more.

I remember how destitute I felt. I was so hungry that I even considered eating seaweed. But instead, I tried every door of every car, found many of them unlocked and raided every glove compartment. After a meagre meal of two bars of fusty chocolate, a packet of stale crisps and a whole box of Fox's glacier fruits, I climbed back into Constantin's caravan, drank a potion made from something called sea holly for those who "lack delight," and fell asleep immediately.

Sometimes I wonder about that evening and try to imagine what would have happened if I had just started walking back along the road until I reached a bus stop, a train station or at least a place where I could have bought some food. But I didn't. I couldn't.

That night, my daughter, I dreamed of you. I don't want to sound sentimental or, even worse, wilfully insane, but to tell you exactly what happened. Even though I could never have imagined you then, I saw you high up on a wire walking towards your father. Your face was older than its baby self but your hair was still the colour of pale silver. I called out to you to be careful. You did not fall.

I am spooked by her words, full of jitters, freaked out. A real father simply complicates matters. I had not thought that far, not recently, not since The Great Barrissimo broke my heart when he told me I wasn't his even though he wished I were.

She knows nothing. I slam the pages shut and throw her manuscript to the ground where it lands with a thump and a small puff of dust. I did fall. I fell. Or maybe I'm still falling. Isn't that how it is? Isn't that how it feels when death is below and life is above and time slows down so your slide through the air takes years instead of seconds. Isn't that how it is?

Breakfast: one cup of tea, one Fry's Peppermint cream, half an over-ripe banana and a handful of peanuts. The shop at the bottom of my block has closed down. Julie has stopped coming. Today I am being visited by F. McLorn (Miss). At 10 A.M. In fifteen minutes.

Rap, rap. Rararrap. It is 9.45 A.M. The knock on the door has an amused kind of style. She's early. Unforgivable. I know I will hate her.

"It's open," I shout. What kind of burglar would come up to the 36th floor with no lift? Is she an idiot?

F. McLorn (Miss) wears too much lipstick. It looks as though she has just stroked it on outside my door, leaving it all sticky and gummy-looking. Her hair is neither short nor long, but in-between, her clothes are mainly black. Can't commit herself to the personality statement of a colour, clearly.

She is younger than Julie and is only slightly puffed by all the stairs. The shake her hand gives mine is firm, like a man's. And when she looks at me at last, there is something about the distance in her gaze which makes me think that she has judged me already, that she is unethically fascinated by me, that I will provide endless material for telephone conversations to friends in slow periods in the office. And I know that to her I am not a girl at all, but a fascinating dossier in the Problem Cases tray.

"Well now," she says as she opens her briefcase.

Well now what, I ask myself.

"Julie's off sick, so I've come to take over. I see there's been a bit of a communication problem here. But we'll soon sort this out. I'm sure it's all been a wee misunderstanding."

F. talks and talks and talks. I lose interest after the first minute, switched off by words like rights and benefits and statuary this and statuary that. It seems, like the tower block, I, too, am condemned by bureaucracy. When I listen again, I hear the words forcible eviction and finally understand that they will try and make me leave the day after tomorrow.

"Everything's changed," I say, suddenly. "I've had a letter from an uncle I never knew I had. He's coming to pick me up. "

F. sighs. She doesn't believe me. Compulsive liar must be written in my file too.

"It's the same situation for everyone who lives here," she says.

But I have drifted off again and become fixated on the split end of a single hair. And then she taps me, hard, on the knee, as if I am a door.

"The welfare system does provide a net for cases like yours," she says. "That's what it's for."

"I never work with nets," I say. "Too easy to get strangled."

"The support facilities are all there," she says. "It's up to you. I'm happy to show you."

"I'm not going anywhere with you," I say.

She pauses and I can almost hear her counting from one to ten. I've infuriated her. Good.

"You know you may hold up the building programme. Cost the taxpayer millions of pounds. The shopping and leisure centre was scheduled to open by the Millennium. It's already very late."

"Oh, you should have said earlier," I say, my sarcasm prompting a long low sigh. At least there is some response at last.

F. McLorn is far worse than Julie. She stays for hours; she does not seem to want to leave. She asks me to sign bits of paper, which I won't. She asks me personal questions, which I ignore. She advises me to see a psychiatrist. I turn on the television, which is something I never do. And then I sit and watch anything, anything to make her go away.

"To make a delicious leg of lamb with a rosemary crust," says a woman with a bright blue apron and baggy eyes, "first trim all the fat from the meat."

Blood and flesh fill the screen. Fingers dissecting, a knife gently serrating, pale pink and off-white.

"Who was your mother?" the social worker's voice says.

I am suddenly moved. Moved into my mother's story. Helena standing on the edge of the sea. How did she get to the other side? Was she pushed or did she jump? But hell, bugger, damn, what do I care, I ask myself. Why did I read all her stuff? It has only confused me more. I don't need her now. I am alone.

"Now, and this is the fun bit," the television instructs. "Take it in both hands and roll it in the seasoned bread crumbs. Try and give it a really good massage, a nice firm caress."

"Hey," interrupts F. McLorn. "Are you listening to me? You're not a child anymore. Did you hear me?"

There is only a small click when F. McLorn leaves. I barely hear it until minutes later. She has left her business card on the table.

Chapter seven

Sleat Rock

You have every right to be furious with me, my little daughter. I wasn't there for you in the physical sense, just in spirit, which isn't quite the same thing. But as you will discover it was not deliberate. Even though it is a different scenario entirely, I know how you must feel. And even though the circus performaers did not know I was there, I too felt rejected that evening. Forsaken, dumped, abandoned.

In the middle of the night I was woken by the approaching sound of vague and insistent roaring. It was the rumble of not one, but two cars being pushed beyond their capacity and driven extremely fast. Due to the echo of the high sides of mountain and deep slab of water, at first it was hard to tell if they were on this shore or on the other. But soon, sooner than I was prepared for, they screeched to a halt beside the deserted circus encampment, their headlights blaring into the darkness of my sleep.

I didn't move, but lay and listened to the noise of engines revved for fun. And then the car doors opened, a bottle smashed on a stone and I heard the timbre of recently broken voices, intoxicated and silly. I knew what boys of that age were like. I'd seen plenty of them during my time at Valentine's. Individually, they were probably polite and well behaved, but together, they were unpredictable and dangerous.

They walked around the camp, bursting open the doors of the caravans one by one. My door was locked but I knew they would be drawn to the new vehicle with the orange trim eventually and there was nowhere in the small space of Constantin's caravan to hide. I crept quickly out of bed and crawled along the floor. Under the bed, there was a large, dark furry mass. It was the bear costume. Suddenly some dust gathered in my nose and I sneezed, twice. A deadening silence descended. Then a loud giggle came from quite near, followed by the splintering of wood.

It was a pathetic idea, but in situations such as that, you do not think of the originality or plausibility. Wriggling and fumbling with the poppers, zips and ties, I hurriedly slipped the costume on. It was far too big and wrinkled in bunches at the ankles and fell over my hands like a religious jumper.

And then, for I knew I had to make the first move, I unlocked the door, stepped out of the caravan and tried to lumber the way bears do. I could not see much out of the eyeholes for, although my head was too small, I was almost blinded by fear. Any second, I thought, I will feel the blow of a blunt instrument; any second now I would be assaulted or worse.

But nothing happened. Instead I heard the sound of half a dozen sharp intakes of breath, panicked footsteps and the slamming of doors as the boys hastily retreated. It had worked. My impression must have been truly and menacingly bear-like, if a little on the small side, and as the engines spluttered to a start, I felt triumphant for the first time in months and even attempted a bear-like thumping of the chest.

The cars skidded on the grass and accelerated so fast their wheels screamed. Only when they had receded into the distance, did I stand up straight and pull off my mask. But the relief I felt soon vanished. The silence they left behind was even more terrifying than the noise they had made. It held the cries of wild things and the snap and rush of strange night creatures. I was used to cities and villages, places with streetlights and illuminated shop signs, not miles of dark sea and even darker, denser land. The boys' fear lingered in the air, the mad, irrational terror of the unknown. To make it worse, I was suddenly struck with the thought that they might come back again in greater numbers, armed with guns and torches. The lights of the house across the sound fell in a white rippling path. Somehow I had to cross the water.

The rocks on the shore were slippery with seaweed and slime. In the light of the setting moon, I could almost see my way but not well enough. I jumped from bleached rock to bleached rock, look-ing, I suppose in vain for a boat. But my bear feet were soon sodden and as I tried to leap across a small inlet, I skidded and I lost my balance.

It all happened so slowly; the rush of weightlessness, the fleet-ing thrill when I caught sight of the water below and then the shock as the sea swallowed me whole. I had fallen, head over heels over the sheer, black edge. At first the chill pulled my breath away. It was so cold, I thought I would die then and there. But instead I sank slowly down, down towards the bottom of the cold, cold sea.

I opened my eyes. The water was deeper than it looked. I saw the black fur of the costume fan out all around me like a sea anemone. Below, seaweed frayed full deep green and flashed with the bolt of silver fish. Far up above, I could see the moon through the rippling lens of the water's surface. Spangled bubbles rose slowly upwards like tiny glass baubles. How, I asked myself, could I manage to see anything? It was night, it was dark, but the water was almost luminescent. Somehow, I had fallen into the wide throw of light from the house.

And then I noticed that gradually, very gradually the cur-rent was pulling me away from the shore and into deeper water. In the clumsy thickness of the sea, I tried to pull poppers, unzip zips and struggle out, but the bear outfit was too heavy, too big. The costume held me in its fabric embrace and slowly, as slow as the

Angel's Descent, I was heading to the murky black depths of the very bottom.

This, I thought, is it. No one knows I'm here. I'm alone. I'm sinking. I'm dying. I thought of my parents, of Milo, Clara, Mortimer and finally of Constantin as the light all around me glittered like a million missing sequins. Somehow, it was rather beautiful. And even though I was only seventeen, I had to remind myself to mind. But when I did, I minded. I minded a lot. But with every kick of my heels, every swing, every flail of my body made in its hairy shroud, the world I knew seemed to recede into the past tense.

That night I had already dreamed of tightropes. As I sunk deeper, I looked up and caught a glimpse of what I thought was a nude acrobat balancing on the light of the surface far, far above. I couldn't have seen that distance through the warp of so much water, but there he was, clear and distinct, a man on a rope pulled tight. Hesitatingly he crossed foot by foot, his balance unsure, his concentration visible, and then, in one naked arc, he fell. Or should I say, he leapt.

There are some things, my dear that I cannot explain. The man was Constantin and somehow he pulled me up from the bottom of the sea and into his boat. The logistics of it were quite straightforward. He had woken at the sound of car engines, watched what had happened through a telescope from the island and had seen my highly effective bear-impersonation and my accidental plunge into the sea. But you may be thinking that it must have taken him at least ten minutes to reach the spot where I had fallen and then another five to locate me.

I know that by then I should have been technically dead. The water was cold enough to kill in under a minute. But I lived. You may wonder if I have wandered off the plot completely into the realms of fantasy and make-believe, but I swear to you that this whole episode is true.

As I lay in the boat, Constantin stripped off yards of sodden fake fur and then held me skin to skin, his naked body next to mine and his warm breath on the back of my neck. First he hugged and rubbed me and then he took both my cold blue feet and clutched them under his armpits. It was a desperate routine that local fisher women used to perform on drowned sailors. I was aware of what was happening and yet I was unaware that the close-to-dead girl was me. I watched in pure distracted detachment as Constantin rowed back to the island with tears streaming down his moon-pallored face.

Clumsily, he carried me up a small path, through some dense black yew trees and into the large house. In a room completely dark apart from the last embers of a smouldering log fire he laid me down in a large and scratchy armchair and covered me with as many blankets and quilts as he could find. And then I listened to the strange but distinctive sounds of a flame being lit, metal pounding on metal and air blown through water, until I fell once more, this time into a deep, dreamless sleep.

Days later, I was not sure then how many, I woke up. I lay in a bed under a huge red candlewick bedspread in a room on the first and only remaining floor of a tower. There was a fire smoking in the grate and a candle on the mantelpiece but that was all, no pictures, no furniture and no carpets. The shutters at the window flaked with green paint and there was a small metal bowl on the floor to catch the rain from a hole in the roof.

My hands lay over the bedspread and looked like the hands of a medieval lady on a church tomb. The night spent with Constantin in his orange camper van seemed very long ago and the purple circle on my right hand had disappeared completely. Constantin sat dozing beside me, his head bowed towards an open book on his lap. I watched him for a minute, saw large dark rings beneath his closed eyes and the scrabble of a beard and wondered how long I had been there.

With all my strength, I sat up. But rather than feeling the fantastic surge of life that the newly saved are often reported to feel, I leaned over the edge of the bed and before I could stop myself I had vomited all over the floor. Constantin woke up and almost leapt out of his seat in surprise.

"Sorry," I said.

"Hello," he said. "Don't worry. It's just the side-ways effects."

You would not believe the remedy of plants, metals and other ingredients that he had administered to me. I discovered later that it included several poisons of the most extreme kind. Whatever they were, however, they seemed to have worked.

"You're still here," Constantin whispered the first day after I woke.

"Why yes," I said indignantly, for initially I misunderstood what he meant.

But as the realisation of how close I had been to death dawned, I felt quite weak. I spent my time wrapped up in warm wool blankets and thick socks, saying very little. I also had vague flashbacks of hearing voices, arguments and raised whispers and knew that the other members of Ursa Major were camping out somewhere in the house. Their caravans still huddled in a cluster on the other side of the sound, but a stifled laugh from behind a door, a throaty cough or a lingering odour of something resembling gun powder revealed that the four Masters of Matter, Fanny the female magician and Magnus the ringmaster were still all there.

Later, I heard that they had argued so badly about my condition that they had almost come to blows. Magnus had wanted to ship me back to the mainland and take me to hospital, but Constantin had refused point-blank.

Slowly I regained my composure. Slowly I began to piece together what had happened to me. Slowly I began to take in my surroundings. The first thing I noticed was the wind. On the night of my arrival, it seemed it had been unusually calm, unseasonably fair. But it soon transpired that this was a temporary lull. For by the time I awoke, the wind had returned with such omnipotent force that it was hard to imagine the island without it.

Howling through the eaves, it was as much part of the landscape as the grass, the heather or the exposed rock. This wind wasn't a noise you grow used to such as the ticking of a clock. Sometimes it dropped and would seem to pause and rest but then it would build up and up again and churn and moan like a washing machine at full speed spin cycle until you were quite desperate for peace, quite desperate for absolute still.

In fact, it seemed to be trying to blow down the house. And it had, in some ways, already made a significant impact. I suspect it was more the fault of the bog on to which the house was built but every wall tilted, every floor sloped and while on the west side the ground floor windows were so high up it was impossible to see through them, on the east, they had become low doorways the right height for dwarves.

The other thing I couldn't help but notice was the damp. I recognised that mouldy aroma straight away. Our house on the side of the hill had boasted areas which my father insisted, "needed airing," such as the cellar and the back bathroom, but they were nothing like this. Everything was constantly sticky to the touch, everything smelled. Even, I discovered to my horror, me. It was in the air, you swallowed it and felt it settle inside you like fog, it was underfoot; it was in your hair, dripping, sopping, and phlegmish damp. No amount of heat could make you ever feel dry enough; no amount of blankets could ever make you feel warm enough. Honestly, I felt as if I was becoming aquatic.

But I didn't care. Not then, anyway. Three times a day Constantin brought me hot tea and a plate of porridge with honey. And then he would sit down and we would either talk or he would perform for me, making sprigs of heather burst into bright green flames or exploding apples in the garden below.

"Watch this," he'd shout before he carried out some trick. "Watch out!" he'd yell, when a piece of singed fruit flew through the window and bounced off my bedroom roof.

And then, once I had laughed so much I hurt all over again, I'd look down at the top of his head with its black, black hair and clean white parting and wish I knew all there was to know about him. You see, although he would happily talk about the island, Sleat Rock, its geological make up—metamorphic slate formed in the Precambrian period, just in case you're interested—every time I asked him about his past, about where he had come from or where he had learned such wonderful tricks, he changed the subject or insisted he create another spectacular sight for me alone.

One evening I would not let it go.

"Where?" I insisted.

"Are you feeling feverish?" he asked and placed his huge hand on my brow. "Fiddlededee, you're hot."

"From the north…?"

He frowned.

"From the east?"

He sighed and smoothed down the faded blankets on my bed.

"Go to sleep," he said softly.

But I'd guessed, you see. I recognised his accent, the way he rolled his consonants with his tongue. And hadn't his nickname been Boris at Valentine's?

"Dushka," I said softly.

He turned and looked at me, his eyes suddenly glassy in the flickering candlelight.

"You don't know what you're saying," he said.

Actually it was true, I had no idea, but I had heard Clara saying the same phrase to Milo.

"You're Russian," I said.

The air seemed to pause all around him, the still night held its breath, the sea momentarily stopped its relentless churning, and even the wind died. His head tipped back, very slightly and his lips parted, just a little, before he spoke.

"Da," he replied. "Nu kakoy zhe tiy dushka."

Recently I looked up Clara's phrase. And then I understood, in part, why he was so surprised. "Darling," was the Russian word Clara often used to purr to Milo. Maybe after all, love was more to her than a lie to make life more bearable.

One day I woke up and felt completely recovered. I hadn't been out since my fall into the sea, and was growing restless from being cooped up in bed with that taste of fungus in my mouth. I was fed up of convalescing, tired of being talked to like a child, quite sick of being stuck in that room all day with the wind going round and round the house like a spool of cotton unwinding.

"I'm going out." I said. "Today. Now in fact. And don't try and stop me."

Through the hole in the roof and the slats of the shutters, which were kept closed because the window was broken, I could see clouds racing by. It was a clear afternoon, cold, sunny and of course, blustery. Constantin, however, was reluctant.

"Stick to the paths," he said. "Wear this. And this. And this. Promise me you won't go to the eastern shore because the path is unsafe and don't be too long."

Outside, my hair danced above my head and whipped into my face. I wore two coats, borrowed and strange smelling. Walking into the wind at an angle, I followed the path that ran round the island and reached a rocky shore. Yellow lichen and green barnacles covered every boulder and tiny white crabs scuttled into rock pools. On the western side, where the wind raced straight off the Atlantic and made my eyes stream with tears, I discovered a cliff-enclosed semi-circle of white sand. In the middle, its curve half-covered by a small dune, was the bleached backbone of a whale.

Although my childhood home was only a matter of hours drive away, I felt as if I was in a different world. The sky was bigger and the island looked so wild it was doubtful whether the path I trod had been stepped on by more than a handful of people. Ever.

The centre of Sleat Rock was bog land pierced with oily pools and tufted with clumps of coarse grass. Right in the middle, at the base of the hillock was a half-sunken Celtic cross placed there by Saint Columba on his way to the island of Iona. No wonder he hadn't stayed. He too, like me, was probably quite dishevelled by wind and he had most likely squelched through mud until his legs, up to the knees, were as brown and slimy as mine.

I climbed the steep slope behind the cross, stood on the highest point and looked over towards the mainland. A couple of cars threaded their way along the road. A small rowing boat was bobbing alongside the jetty. By the bright red wig, I recognised Mr Air. From a distance I could see that my temporary home was a medieval tower with a house stuck rather clumsily on one side. Both were falling apart with slates missing from the roof, crumbling masonry and cracked, dirty windows.

From here the extent of the disintegration was obvious. The house had once been quite substantial, with three floors, around twenty rooms and dozens of smaller pantries, bathrooms and cloakrooms. But now it was a ruin. We only used the kitchen at the back of the house and the connecting parlour to eat and sit in. The other rooms didn't have any glass in their windows.

Then something caught my eye, something down on the eastern shore where I was not allowed to go. I saw the distinctive ruffle of brown and a rambling gait. It was probably a large bird, I told myself, a capercaillie, perhaps, or an overweight puffin. On the island there were birds everywhere, gulls which hovered in the slipstream like ticks against the great white sky, oyster catchers which stalked the shore and tiny finches and sparrows, diving and swooping through the grass or trilling in alarm at the sound of my approach.

As for the house, the eaves, chimneys and gutters were home to so many species of roosting birds that it often seemed as if humans were the intruders rather than the other way around. There were also mice, rats, spiders and wood lice, plus so many dust mites, that whenever you reclined on the various ancient sofas and armchairs, they would rise up in a great cloud.

As I gazed down, I remember asking myself why anyone would choose to live here. Whatever secrets the Ursa Major circus held, they had come to the very edge of the earth to make sure they were kept. It was the end of the road, a place to hide, a place to disappear.

The wind blew and blew right through my clothes and seemed to twist itself around my bones. I was cold right through. I hadn't bathed for days. I'd even forgotten what I looked like.

In front of me was a long slope covered in bracken, and partly to warm myself up and partly because I suddenly felt a wave of nostalgia for the child I once was and the place I used to live, I threw up my arms and started to run down the hill, stumbling and rolling, racing and freewheeling until I knew the only thing which could stop me was the bottom.

I reached the back door of the house quite out of breath. A large fire was roaring in the grate. An old lead bath stood in front of it and from its surface rose swirls of steam. As I pulled off various coats, scarves, gloves and hats, Constantin took a pot from the fire and poured more boiling water into the tub.

"I made you a bath," he said and smiled. "I think you need one."

Seeing him again, I remember I felt a distinct rise inside. His face was radiant in the filtered afternoon light. He wore an old fishing jumper, which had huge holes at the elbow, and a pair of old man's trousers. Here he was again, the man who I had held inside like a promise, Constantin, the bear man. We looked, him at me and me at him, and I knew then that I would not leave until he did. Not for anything.

"I hope you don't expect me to strip off right here?" I asked.

With a small bow he fixed an old tartan blanket up between us and left me totally sealed in.

"Take as long as you like," he said from the other side of it. "It is all part of the cure."

I suspected that my recovery had taken a lot longer than I first imagined. Although I could only guess that it was still February, I deduced correctly that I had been in bed for several weeks.

Anyway, that night, wearing the ancient white night-shirt and thick mustard yellow cardigan that I had found in a chest under the bed, (for no one seemed to know what had become of the clothes I had arrived in), I came down the spiral staircase of the tower and into the back kitchen. A spluttering oil lamp hung from a nail on the wall and threw grubby shadows into the corners. On the table were a loaf of bread and a large pot of soup.

Nobody noticed me at first, and so I hovered at the foot of the stairs and watched them. They hadn't changed much since I had seen them last. Mr Fire's long white beard had fallen into his soup bowl and was turning green, Mr Air's belly threatened to burst out of his jacket, and as if to prove the point, a button broke loose and pinged into the bread-basket, and Fanny, the female magician, inhaled on a cheroot and blew blue smoke in rings up to the ceiling.

In the light from the fire, they looked like the oldest people in the world. Magnus's skin was grooved with lines and pits. Dressed in the same greasy dinner jacket as he had been wearing the last time I saw him, with the addition of a huge black jumper and a tartan scarf tied around his neck, Magnus looked more like a scarecrow than a ringmaster. He turned towards me and suddenly, without the light, his eyes seemed to turn pitch black. I jumped, despite myself.

"Aaaagh," he said in his deep, deep voice. "Look who we have here."

The next few minutes were characterised by acute awkwardness on all fronts. I was ushered into a seat next to the fire, a bowl was placed in front of me and then, to everyone's obvious dismay, I was served what was left of the soup.

"We seem," said Mr Fire.

"To have eaten it," said Mr Air.

"All?" said Mr Earth.

"Oh dear," said Fanny. "How dreadfully rude."

But I really wasn't hungry. My knees shook slightly, my breath was shallow, my heart still raced.

"Have mine," said Constantin from the seat beside me. His bowl was untouched. Either he wasn't keen on kelp broth or he wasn't hungry either.

There was so much unsaid, so much implied, so much suggested that it is hard to give an accurate sense of that time. What did we talk about? I can't remember. What jokes did I laugh at? Who knows? Instead, imagine the smell of wood smoke and the crackle of peat, imagine faces red from the fire and mouths which couldn't help smiling despite every effort not to. Imagine the space between

Constantin and me getting smaller and smaller until, without even realising it, our elbows and knees, our thighs and ankles brushed.

"Sorry," I said.

"Sorry," he said. And it must have been so obvious to everyone but us.

Later that night, as we drank a bottle of Claret covered by a thick layer of dust with the date 1932 on the label which had been brought up from the cellar in my honour, they politely but firmly quizzed me. Who was I, where had I come from and when did I think I was going to leave? Up to this point I had no difficulty in responding.

"I thought," I said in a quiet voice. "I mean, as I've already said to… "

I nodded towards Magnus and Constantin. Each looked away, one fiddling with the wine cork and the other, with the frayed collar of his jersey, respectively.

"I want to join Ursa Major," I said.

"Why do you think," said Magnus in a voice that made the wine bottle rattle. "That the answer is any different from our initial response?"

"Wait," interrupted Constantin. "Not now. Please."

Fanny and the Masters of Matter were clearly confused. Looks flew back and forth across the table.

"Oh dear!" said Fanny. "Well, this changes things entirely."

"Entirely," repeated Mr Earth.

"Well anyway, even if it were possible, we are not going out again. Not for a very long time, at least." Magnus looked at me, his gaze as dense as treacle.

"As you may have gathered, we are natural scientists and we are about to embark on a period of research and experimentation."

"I'll wait," I said.

Our conversation was broken by a loud crash, as one of the few remaining windows was blown in by the wind. Had we continued it then what happened next might not have taken place. But the subject was left hanging like the empty window frame from one remaining hinge. And as we gathered up the pieces of broken glass from the floor and I cut my finger, I knew from the way they spoke to me and instructed me in the art of handkerchief bandaging, that they did not believe I would last a minute on Sleat Rock. But they were wrong.

Chapter eight

The Stumbling Days

Although their appearance was eccentric to say the least, there was nothing immediately untoward about the Ursa Major ensemble. Yes, their hands were stained strange colours, not just the yellow of nicotine, but green, orange and purple. And they did often smell pungently of something I can only compare to radiators switched on for the first time in winter. The longer I stayed, however, the more uncomfortable they appeared to be. And likewise, the longer I remained, the more uncomfortable they seemed to want to make me feel.

Little Wing, you might know this, then, later, when you read this all grown up. There are some places that when you arrive, when you step off the bus, or alight from a train, you feel like you're stepping into the future. It's not just the architecture or the quality of people's clothes or hairstyles but something intangible, such as the texture of the air or the taste of the light. And it's as if you're standing both in the present and in a place years from that moment, as if you have fallen forward, not vertically but horizontally until you feel the queasy jolt of some kind of internal vertigo.

The island of Sleat Rock was the opposite of that. Being there was as if I had been yanked backwards. Every day when I woke up, I grew increasingly uncertain that I had ever lived in a city at all. Only the sporadic traffic on the other side of the sound proved that it was indeed the second half of the twentieth century and not the nineteenth, eighteenth or even the seventeenth. At first I saw it almost like a challenge, after all, my old home on the hill hadn't been exactly palatial. But it was such a lot of work.

The house on the island was the property of Mr McPhee, or so it said on the post-box at end of the small wooden jetty. Why, I asked myself at the time, would a Scottish Laird let his house be squatted in by a group of threadbare circus performers? Where was he? Of course it took a lot of effort to extract even the most meagre bit of information.

"Who is Mr McPhee?" I asked Constantin one morning as he stirred a huge vat of volcanic porridge.

"That's Magnus," he replied as he sprinkled a handful of salt in to the pot.

"You mean he owns this island?" I went on.

"In the name of the wee man will you stop asking me questions and lay the table," he said. "Now make way, make way for breakfast."

The porridge, or should that be gruel (for we had no milk), ran out long before Constantin's patience. As did the honey. In fact, as well as having no electricity and no hot water, we soon ran out of all essential supplies. As my stay on Sleat Rock lengthened, I became increasingly hungry. And not just for information. When Fanny brought a pot of seaweed soup, again, to the table, I sighed loudly.

"Is this all there is?" I asked.

Fanny put down the ladle on the table and gathered up her hands in front of her.

"Why don't you cook tomorrow?" she said. "And then you can make anything you like."

"Okay," I said. "I will."

It was almost spring but still the cold seemed to seep under doors and creep round the blankets hung over the windows to keep in the warm. The weather and my growing hunger, however, were simply a minor distraction. On my mind, most of the time, was Constantin. I used to follow him around the house like a lap dog, throwing myself down on one of the ancient sofas when he stretched out on a scuffed chaise lounge to read a book and then leaping up again when he rose minutes later. He was, however, adept at escaping and regularly gave me the slip in the huge house with its multiple interconnecting rooms.

Indeed, it was indicative of my emotional state that on that day I wandered into the kitchen full of ideas for dinner, I considered fish à l'orange. Fanny was sitting at the large, warped table that curled up at each end like an Arabian slipper, bashing the life out of a piece of dough. When I told her my plans, she laughed, not unkindly, and opened the cupboard. Inside was one onion, a packet of mouldy biscuits and half a sack of flour, which, I was horrified to witness, wriggled with weevils.

"Insects," I cried.

"I wouldn't be too outraged," she said. "You've been eating them for weeks."

Then she handed me a large pot.

"How about a nice nettle and mussel stew," she suggested. "I saw a patch of mussels just down on the shore beside the jetty. And there are heaps of nettles in the garden."

I had no idea. I thought that they had cooked strange frugal meals because they liked them. I had imagined a larder stocked with tins like my parents. Three hours later, when it was getting dark outside, I returned. My fingers were raw and numb with cold and my legs were covered in scratches and stings. Fanny looked into the pot disdainfully. My collection was pitiful, not enough to feed one, let alone eight.

"There must be something else," I said. "Surely there must be more food somewhere."

But there wasn't. We ate one mussel each and a couple of soggy nettle leaves that night. And the next. And the next. Sometimes I felt the former members of Ursa Major's eyes on me, saying Go, Go, Go! And they were so patronising, what with their details of new fast food restaurants opening on the mainland or their talk of different kinds of chocolate. Sometimes I thought of taking the boat and going shopping on the mainland. But I sensed that once I stepped off the island I would never be able to come back. Magnus would take care of that, some way or another. And so, rather than going quietly, the way they wanted me to, I stayed.

One night, whispering voices outside woke me. I looked out of the window and saw the Masters of Matter, Magnus, Fanny and finally Constantin pass below me in single file. They were heading towards the winding path that led up the small hillock behind the house. The moon was full that night and I could see them all quite clearly. In his hand Magnus held a small metal bowl. Mr Water cradled a vial of liquid. I watched them as they climbed the incline and then clustered at the top. After only a minute or two, a white flash briefly illuminated their faces. And then down they came again, taking it in turns to hold the bowl.

The next day everyone came to breakfast looking distinctly pleased with themselves. Clearly something had happened. But nobody would admit anything.

"What were you doing last night?" I hissed to Constantin as I dried up the bowls he washed. "I saw you all climbing the hill behind the house."

"I don't think so," he said. "You must have dreamt it."

The steam from the sink misted up the filthy window above. Constantin's hair hung in limp spirals across his face. I leaned over to his ear and whispered,

"I know I didn't."

He jumped so violently that five plates flew out of his hands and smashed on the cracked white porcelain of the Belfast sink.

"Bugger!" he yelled.

I am sure I tormented him. He was just as aware of my presence as I was of his. It was just that while I stoked up my fire, he kept trying to blow his out.

"Where do you all go to all day?" I asked him one morning as he was trying to light a fire made of chunks of smoking peat.

"Helena," he replied. "I've been thinking. Don't you have school to go to?"

"No," I replied. "I left years ago... Please tell me."

"I think I shall take you back to the mainland tomorrow. This is no place for a young girl."

"Not yet. Please?"

And then I would cough, pathetically, consumptively, innocently, and that would make him abandon whatever he was doing, come to me, wrap a blanket around me and forget everything I had just said.

Sometimes, to keep me quiet, plans for another tour way, way ahead in the distant future were discussed. New tricks were performed strictly, it was obvious, for my benefit. Occasionally, however, I would hear a loud bang from the other half of the house or notice a particularly pungent smell blown through the shutters by the wind. I knew that something was going on. At the time, however, I couldn't imagine what it could be.

Bit by bit, however, I began to piece things together. I dreamt of the room that I had been taken to and vividly remembered the light of the fire, the strange taste of Constantin's concoctions and the sense of event. Despite a half-hearted attempt at role-playing circus performers, they were no good at deception. I asked them about places, about tricks, about whether they knew people I knew, but all they gave me were inane grins. When they claimed that a circus ring could be 30 feet wide if it felt like it, I knew that none of them had ever performed in a real big top. Everyone knows it has to be 42 feet in diameter. Anything less and the centrifugal force is so strong that a bareback rider can't stand up on his horse.

"What's going on?" I remember asking one day when I noticed something burning which definitely wasn't wood.

"On," said Mr Fire. "Nothing."

"But that smell?"

"My dear girl," said Mr Fire. "You have a more vivid nasal imagination than me."

And every day after the same frugal breakfast, they all trooped off one by one, giving different excuses but all heading to the same place. I watched them.

When I found the library, it reinforced my view that Constantin was mixed up in something a little more than unusual than he would admit. From floor to ceiling, and in large wooden boxes stacked a half dozen high, were literally thousands of books. Many were slim volumes bound in leather, but more than half were thick as several telephone directories. I examined the spines. Most of the titles were in Latin but a few were hand-written in English. One was called *The Vanity and Nothingness of Human Knowledge*.

At random I pulled out a volume. Its pages were musty and thin as rice paper and the text was written in Latin. On almost every single page was a diagram of an experiment liberally decorated with dancing skeletons, strange symbols and botanical illustrations of plants. The book looked archaic, a museum piece, which should have been displayed along with bloodletting bulbs. I flicked through the pages and finally twigged that it was for students in some kind of ancient science; alchemy to be exact. Little did I know that the book I was so carelessly flicking through had once been the prized possession of Sir Isaac Newton.

That night at dinner I realised the implications of what they termed as 'leakage' and the gravitas with which they worked.

"There's no more bread?" asked Mr Water.

"Why don't you just magic some up?" I said.

In the silence my remark created, my fork rattled down on my plate like the crash of a cymbal.

"What?" said Magnus. "What did you say?"

"Only joking," I added.

How could they have thought I would go quietly? The more reticent and suspicious they were, the more daring I became. In retrospect I believe that Constantin couldn't stand all the pretence.

And how could he hide his one vocation? It was as much part of him as the colour of his hair. I know that now. But I wasn't supposed to know. And he wasn't allowed to tell me.

The next morning I followed Constantin and Magnus through the house, up some stairs, out along the roof of the Georgian building and down into a small sloping hallway with a broken skylight.

A wooden door had been left slightly ajar at the other end. It led into a much larger chamber. I crept across and looked through the crack. A metal press stood in the corner with a giant screw like an oversized nutcracker. On a table were half a dozen glass beakers filled with liquid of various shades of dark green. Another filled with clear liquid bubbled gently above a small flame, and in the middle of the room was a furnace complete with a bashed, blackened oven and a set of battered leather bellows. Elsewhere I noted bottles and jam-jars, each labelled with tiny writing, and a stack of used utensils piled haphazardly in the sink.

It was a laboratory, not of the white, sterile, modern, science classroom type, but one fitted out with ancient equipment, naked flames and bristling with a sense of expectation.

The Masters of Matter and Fanny were already there. There seemed to have been some disagreement about quantities, for Mr Air was standing in the centre of the room saying, "I told you so, I told you so…ONE teaspoon. Not TWO." He repeated this over and over again while Fanny and Mr Fire took it in turns to stir a crucible full of liquid.

"It's not my fault," said Mr Fire. "If only someone hadn't misplaced the blasted book."

I peeked further and noticed that the test-tube was boiling over, spilling hot frothy liquid all over the floor.

"Stage Four. Ruined," proclaimed Mr Air.

"No, I wouldn't say that," said Magnus. "Let's try and work out a way to remedy the situation."

And then they all stood in silence and stared at the test-tube. I must say, I couldn't see quite why they were so upset. Little did I know that it had taken them six weeks to reach that particular stage including the aforementioned trip at midnight to the highest point of the island to take advantage of the full moon's polarised light. What were they doing? Right then, I had no idea.

But their activities, no matter how unusual, bizarre or misguided, were soon shelved in my mind. As I said, I grew hungrier and hungrier; I reconsidered taking the boat to the mainland. But the weather had turned stormy and the sea would have swallowed up the boat like a minnow. And so I spent whole days on the shore looking for anything edible.

Inland, at Fanny's instruction, I'd collect a variety of leaves from plants I had never even noticed before. Weeds, basically. These were shredded and boiled up to make a kind of broth or at a push, chopped up into an unappetising salad. As we slowly worked our way through the sack of flour, Fanny added fermenting apples, which she had found rotting beneath a tree or spices she'd discovered at the back of the cupboard. As you can imagine, the results were revolting. But I ate anything that was put in front of me.

And still spring didn't come. Quite often I would wake up to find the whole coast opposite had completely disappeared behind a wall of fog. It came down from the mountains and unrolled before dawn until it seemed to hover above the sea like smoke. Somehow, although I knew it was simply an illusion, its dense whiteness surrounded the island, cocooning and wrapping us up until I almost imagined that we had snapped off the world and floated away.

The climate seemed to echo my state of mind: I had lost any sense of distance, perspective or reason. Even the behaviour of the others began to seem normal. Maybe it was I, I wondered, who was out on a limb. Maybe I was the one who was acting strangely. And looking back, I'm sure I was. But what could induce six grown men and a woman to live in squalor and near starvation? Something akin to madness, something worth risking everything for.

My little girl, right now you are fast, fast asleep in your cot. You look so right, so utterly right, so utterly sure that you should be here in this moment. And the sight of you with your arms thrown back above your head and your belly full of milk makes me ache. We are born with the expectation that we will be loved. We can't help it. Did I tell you that one night, long after I had recovered, I woke up to find him, Constantin, at my bedside, gazing down at me.

"What?" I asked him sleepily.

"You cried out," he whispered. "I just came to check."

You see, I knew. I knew it was only a matter of time. And he must have known it too. All I had to do was make sure we didn't die of malnutrition before we could admit it.

I soon lost all track of the weeks and months I had been living on Sleat Rock but winter seemed to go on and on. The sea spun with currents and during a particularly fierce storm, the boat was blown from the jetty where someone had carelessly left it moored, and smashed on the rocks.

One night, snow fell. Then the pipes froze and I had to pull up all our water from a well beneath a paving stone at the back of the house. In the mornings I often had to break the ice on the surface. On one such trip I met Magnus. His gaze lingered on my raw, grazed knuckles.

"Had enough yet?" he said.

"Enough? What do you mean?"

"You can leave anytime you like," he replied.

"But the boat… The boat was wrecked in the storm."

"There is another boat…"

His eyes never left my face. Not once did they even blink. Behind him the rotten eaves dripped green ice. Instead of a path, a brown trail of sludge led from the well to the back door. The thought of a warm bath and clean clothes suddenly raced through my chill-befuddled brain. Oh yes, part of me told another part: Yes, yes, yes! But then I happened to notice the expression on Magnus's face.

"You are all going as well?" I asked. "You don't mean just me?"

My voice sounded younger than I wanted it to. Magnus breathed in so deeply he seemed to inhale me. And then I knew that he had no intentions of leaving Sleat Rock. None whatsoever.

"If you're staying then so am I," I replied and shouldered the buckets of water past him. "I'm fine. Fine."

Anyway, this time nature was on my side. It wasn't so much a matter of will, more a matter of time. Because quite suddenly, like the lifting of a curtain in another room, spring came. One day when I wasn't even looking, I noticed tiny leaf buds on trees and the delicate poke of snowdrops in the grass. The air, so long filled with the smell of damp and decay, drifted with the raw green smell of growing things. Plants I hadn't even noticed before seemed to come alive and untwirl with flowers. Beside the back door a bush with bright pink blooms burst dizzily into colour.

I watched it all and was amazed. Sometimes I imagined that I too had grown a long green root, which twisted into the thick black earth of the island. The thrum of my heart was so strong I almost believed I was about to flower too.

Then, one day, when the wind was so mild it felt warm, I walked along the shore. I saw the bob of something large in the shallow bay off the western beach. I could just about make out the blonde struts of a wooden crate. By the time I reached it, other crates were being washed up too, like strange angular turtles. I waded into the sea and then little by little, for they were heavy, I managed to drag them one by one up on to the sand. The lids were nailed down so I broke one open with a rock. I lifted up the splintering wood and there inside, nestling in their bed of straw, were half a dozen pineapples.

I pulled out a fruit and ripped my nails through the scaly skin almost to convince myself that I was not hallucinating. And then I took a bite. Inside it was a bright, succulent, vivid yellow. I held it to my face and sucked in its peppery sweet juice. I had never eaten pineapple that didn't come from a tin before. It dribbled all over my chin and down my sleeves and made my mouth ring. I greedily ate a second and a third until I was completely gorged.

The other crates were also packed with pineapples. I buried my nose in the straw and smelled heat and steamy forests and laughter. I took a fruit in each pocket and ran back to the house. This news was too good to hold in, too good to wait until supper to break. And so I leapt two steps at a time up the stairs to the supposedly 'secret' laboratory. But a few steps short of the door, my eyes level with the gap underneath, I hesitated. Inside I saw feet, feet pacing, pausing, and stamping. Something was going on.

"Blllaargh," exclaimed Constantin from within. "Must we keep talking about this... again? She doesn't know anything."

"You shouldn't have saved her," said Magnus. "Her fate was nothing to do with us... and now... think of the leakage. When we are so, so close."

And then he said something so softly I couldn't make it out. Inside I could see Constantin's feet as he threw himself into a huge leather armchair. One of them tapped the floor, tap, tap... tap, tap.

"It is the only solution," I heard Magnus say. "She has seen too much already. And we are close now, so close."

"But she saw the circus. In fact, lots of people saw the circus."

"You know that was amateur stuff, Constantin, mere home-opathy... this morning we shall try the most dangerous stage of all. The penultimate... You took the oath. Secrecy and celibacy. Never forget that."

Constantin's foot paused. I drew back.

"Of course, you are right," I heard him say.

A silence descended. I felt my eyes begin to prick.

"When?" asked Constantin.

"I have a few ideas," said Magnus. "Don't worry. It shall be quite painless."

I didn't stay long enough to hear Magnus' exact plans. I ran from the attic room, back along the rooftop and down through the house. On the way I passed Mr Air and Mr Water, who looked a little surprised.

Outside I kept on running, stumbling over long grass and tripping over heather, my breath stifling with sobs, and my eyes streaming with tears. Eventually, when I looked around, I found myself on the eastern shore. The sea boiled dark blue. I should have died already, I told myself, what was there to stop me sealing my own fate? I started to pull off my shoes and socks. The sand was clammy and cold beneath my feet. A small wave lapped my toes and I was momentarily shocked by the freezing temperature of the water. When I pulled off my coat, still bulging with pineapples, the wind blew my dress up like a flag.

Suddenly I was aware of a rustling sound coming from a large tree behind me on the shore. It wasn't the shiver of a bird or a squirrel but the heavy tread of a much larger creature. I turned and caught a glimpse of something brown, something big, something furry. Then, from out of an overgrown elderberry tree lumbered the unmistakable shape of a bear. A real bear.

Minutes later when Constantin found me, I was white with rage. I was quite willing in theory to take my own life you see, but I did not want it taken from me by his friends or his blasted bear. In my head I was making plans, run or attack, fight or flee. But nothing had really formulated. Instead, I had started to sing 'Jesus, Clean my Soul,' my voice carried up, up into the strong sea wind. And when he touched my arm, gently, I screamed.

"Will you stop saving me," I said when I had recovered my breath. "I really do not appreciate it. Especially if you're going to kill me."

Right in front of me the bear reared up on its hind legs. And for some reason I did not then apprehend, it started to dance.

"Stop," I yelled.

"It's okay," he said quickly. "It's only Nina."

"WHAT IS GOING ON?!" I shouted and burst into tears. "Up there! In the house. Tell me!"

"Don't ask," Constantin said. "You shouldn't have come. This shouldn't have happened…It has already gone too far."

"But you want to get rid of me," I said. "And the only reason I'm here is you."

"No," he said. "Don't say anymore."

"Let me explain," I insisted. "At least let me do that."

And then I told him in stops and starts what I've told you, about how I ran away from a house full of books and how I escaped a future as a missionary. About what I was doing in Glasgow when I saw him on the dance floor of The Eiffel. And about how I tried to follow him but instead became a member of Valentine's circus and was almost killed in a stunt for which I had no real training. And then I told him I was left behind, but discovered that my old life had gone forever and I explained how I had tried to be ordinary but that I could not forget the way my heart had dived like a bird when we danced. And finally, I admitted to him how I felt when I found him again.

His eyes caught mine and he gazed at me. I knew what he was thinking, I knew that he thought it had all got out of hand.

"Why?" he said.

Why what? To me it was obvious. I picked up his hand, with his fingers all stained with strange colours, and very slowly I stroked it across my cheek.

"Because I've never met anyone like you before. Because you're probably a genius who doesn't know it yet. Because I don't want to lose you again. Because I love you," I said. "Isn't it obvious?"

I forgot the dancing bear, the wind, and the plans that Constantin and his colleagues had been formulating earlier, did not feel the icy wind, leaned closer, stood up on my tiptoes and kissed him on his full red mouth. At first he hesitated. He looked at me with his puzzled expression. But then he blinked, his mouth twirled up at the corners very slightly, one arm sought the small of my back and the other encircled my waist and he kissed me back. Pulled together like the snap of a mussel shell when tapped, we held each other at last.

Mother, mummy, mum, no, no no no NO. I can't swallow that. I don't believe in fairy tales. I can't hear symphonies, not anymore. How old does she think I am? She's too late, always too late, arriving with a loud kerr-flump on my doormat when my days are running out and expecting me to read about kissing on beaches and dancing bears. That's why I have thrown her blasted memoir out with the rubbish, that's why it sailed whiz, whiz, crash down the garbage shoot and into the communal bins where I don't dare go. That's why.

I hope the rats down there have eaten it already. I hope they have. Why should I believe her? She left me. What kind of a mother does a thing like that? What kind of mother was she?

It's the middle of the afternoon. Your light is off. You have gone walking again, over the bridge and underneath the motorway, through the shopping centre and down along the canal where crashed cars poke their bottoms out at the ducks. I've timed your daily walks. Out at twelve and back by five, two plastic bags in each hand, filled with stuff.

The telephone rings. It squeals at me: I'm F. McLorn (Miss) answer immediately! I'm F. McLorn (Miss) answer immediately! And then it stops. And then it starts again. Now! now! it says; Now! Now! It may go on all day. Sometimes my body acts before my head. It always has done. Elsie who took the tickets told me it is something to do with a brain imbalance.

Even though there are rats and mice and dirt and things that hide under rocks in the daylight. Even though there is the smell of rotten, stinking, bad, mouldy, dirty things all scrawled together in one big stink, and even though it is the very bottom of the world, I suddenly decide on a whim to chose my mother's voice over F.McLorn's. Not that I believe her stupid story or anything. Not that I care.

And then the sound of the telephone starts to fade as I start to fly. One, two three, feet first, down the bin chute and black tunnel drop past smeary flaps with numbers… 32… 25… 17… 8… 4… 1… Flip. BANG. Pooooooooooooh.

I hurt. Not much but enough. I am sitting on a pile of rubbish bags ten feet high. It is dark except for a square of light, which comes from a hinged wooden door that opens on to the car park. I try not to breathe in the stink. Something sharp and block-like sticks into my shoulder. I pull it out of its stretchy black cocoon. It is a book. In the weak grey light I read the spine. A Gideon's Bible. Stolen.

But I am not prepared for the squeaky black plastic silence. I am not prepared for the number of bags. What have I done? Will I have to wait for the bin men to come and who maybe won't see me and who will throw me into their mulch machine without noticing my screams? I must find my mother's memoir. Quick before I die of garbage poisoning.

My bag is near the bottom. It smells strongly of fishy tea bags and so carefully I dissect it poking around inside pretending I am not breathing. And yes, it is certainly amazing, especially to cynical old me, but eventually after much rooting and pulling and stuffing, I find the pile of pages attached at the top with a bulldog clip. I find my inheritance again.

But now I am stuck here. Quite stuck. I hear the scratch of rodents. Oh no, oh no, oh no. The time is 4.55 P.M. At two minutes to five exactly, I start to scream, HELP! HELP! HELP!

The daylight darkens like the light has been switched off. There is a man-shaped blob out there in the car park. HELP. It is you. You are standing at the wooden doorway fiddling with the latch. HELP. Your face is hidden by the shadow but you pause for a second when you see me, my head poking out from the small black mountains.

"Hello," I say. "I'm sorry but I'm from flat 36 and I got stuck here accidentally. Could you help me please?"

Your figure shifts and then grows larger as you move towards me. What must you be thinking? That I'm a mad girl who likes to roll in rubbish.

"I can't walk," I say. "I lost the use of my legs in an accident. A pony fell on them and he was heavy, as ponies are, and it took them an awful long time to lift him off. My name is Little Wing."

You don't say anything. Nothing but a small nod. And then you loom over me, your plastic bags of shopping pushed on to your wrists, and you lift me up very gently in your arms. Did you know you smell of fresh air and snow?

The lifts work, my door is open as it always is and you place me on the sofa. I see your eyes take in my living room, my rings, my view, and my flat directly opposite yours.

"Would you like to stay for tea?" I ask. "I have cake. It may be a little stale now but it is the least I could do."

"No," you say your voice quite rusty with age and something else I can't pin down. "No, thank-you."

Your eyes fall on my mother's manuscript in my hand. I roll it tight shut. Private, you see. Even to you. And then, you leave, too quickly, too quickly.

I do not read again for hours. The streetlights start to flash orange in rows across the city and the stars disappear. I sit in the dark and wait for your light to switch on. And then I notice the faint breeze of music in the air. Sleep eludes you too.

It wasn't the cold wind or the presence of a bear that eventually tore us apart. It was an explosion; one almighty crash followed by a low boom. At first I almost believed it was some sort of heavenly timpani, some sort of divine tralala, a personal fanfare. Remember, I had grown up with the sound of dynamite exploding as it blasted away our hill. But Constantin had no such memory and he pulled away, his brow furrowed and his eyes bright with panic.

By the time we reached the house, it was on fire. Black, black smoke poured out of every window while the furious snap of breaking glass, the pop and crack of burning wood and the sound of ripping emitted from deep inside.

Constantin pulled off his coat and before I could stop him, he had rushed through the doorway. Immediately he disappeared behind the streak of falling timber and the lick of bright angry flames. I tried to help. I ran to the well and pulled up bucket after bucket of cold water and kept throwing wide wet arcs at the blaze. But although it was useless—the fire was too fierce, the smoke was too thick—I kept on going.

My arms began to ache. He had been gone too long. The

doorway crashed down in flames. I put down the bucket. The house was burning and I could not stop it. My whole body shook as I bit back my tears. Was life really this cruel? Could we lose each other so soon? Suddenly Constantin stumbled out with Magnus hoisted over his shoulder, alive, but only just. He was about to go back in again, about to cover his head with a blanket and try and save the others but Magnus, with what must have been almost the last of his strength, sat up, grabbed him by the sleeve and then shook his head. It was too late. I could tell from his face. The Masters of Matter and Fanny, the female magician, were all dead.

A loud crash came from the house as the roof fell in. Sparks and debris flew out of the windows. Deep inside, the foundations sighed. The house, so sleepily dormant before, seemed wide-eyed and glorious, lit with a feverish beauty in its final moments.

Only the Gothic tower remained, saved, maybe, by the damp and the direction of the wind. Constantin carried Magnus up the dripping stone steps and laid him on my red bed. His skin was blue and both of his hands were clutched into white-knuckled fists, which he would not relax. With a piece of flint, Constantin lit a small fire in the grate. Everything in his laboratory had been lost: his tinctures, his remedies and his potions; all those books, all that knowledge.

But he still had his notebook, shoved into his back pocket. He carried it everywhere and now rifled quickly through its pages until he came to a scrawled remedy. While I stayed with the former ringmaster, bathing his brow with cool water, Constantin went out to search for ingredients. When he returned, I could tell that something was troubling him. Something was missing. I pulled a pineapple from my pocket. He sighed softly and smiled at me, his face scored with something I had never seen before.

"I found it... on the beach... That was what I was coming to tell you... before..." I blushed.

"Thank you," he said. "Not quite what I need but almost."

All night, Constantin brewed and distilled, chopped and boiled, making new remedies to cure his patient. He placed moss on his forehead and administered juice of dandelion. He covered the ringmaster's white fists with a mixture of pineapple juice and dock leaves. He made him drink a spoonful of foul smelling green liquid every hour. And then we waited, our eyes drawn involuntarily to the billows of black smoke still blotting out the clear night sky.

Apart from the beach, it was the first time we had been alone together, and I mean really alone. Magnus slept, his breath gulped in and then slowly released, and there was no one else alive on the island, no one except Nina the bear.

"I meant what I said earlier," I said eventually, when the silence around us seemed too loud. "Even though I don't understand... you, this, what happened. Tell me who you are and what you were doing here."

"I am not allowed to," he said softly. "I am not allowed."

In the splutter of the fire, I gazed at him, trying to imprint that moment in my memory, trying to keep what I suspected that I might lose.

"Please," I said.

He glanced at me and then looked away. And then right there, as his patient slept and as the night seemed almost endless, he suddenly laughed.

"What does it matter now?" he said. "Everything is gone, everything is lost, my friends are dead. Even the library has gone. How can it possibly matter?"

Without even pausing for breath, he told me. But he was wrong. It did matter. It mattered.

"Have you heard of alchemy," he asked.

I nodded.

"Well I am an alchemist," he said. "What we were doing was the most difficult experiment any alchemist has ever attempted. We were trying to make the Azoth, the Elixir of Life."

He paused.

"The Azoth?" I ventured. "I've heard of it. But I didn't think it actually existed."

"There are six stages. We had reached the fifth. If we had been successful, we could have found a cure for all ailments and would have been able to make gold out of lead."

In some ways his revelation came as a huge relief. He believed in what could be described as a branch of science. But it was more than that and I knew it. What I am trying to say, my dear daughter, is that my instinct about Constantin was right. He was no ordinary man. I also felt a wave of sadness. Right then I didn't know why.

He checked Magnus' brow and when it was clear that there was nothing more he could do for the present, he laid his coat on the floor next to the fire and we sat down. Neither of us spoke for a considerable time.

"Tell me," I whispered eventually. "How? Why?"

"Are you sure you want to know?"

I nodded.

"Very well," he said.

And then as the night stilled in the hours before dawn and the world outside seemed to fall away, he told me.

Chapter nine

Constantin's Tale

Constantin Petrovitch Guershoon was born in Siberia, a place where the winter is never ending and the summer is nothing more than the howl of red dust and a parched white sky. In the forests near his house were bears and wolves. The town where he lived was a small settlement called Nadym. It was at the very end of the railway line. The last stop. He was born in what is known as a Gulag. It was a place where people were sent to disappear.

His parents were originally from Leningrad. She taught children how to play the piano and he was a composer of symphonies. In Siberia, he chopped down trees and she worked in a factory. They played no music but listened to the sound of the wind instead and sometimes told Constantin they heard whole orchestras playing. Sometimes his mother would sing him Chopin or Mozart and teach him the part of the right hand while she would sing the left. His nickname was Medvedik, or Little Bear, because he liked dancing.

His father died the winter when he was six. He was found lying in the street near their house, clutching a bottle of vodka. Although the vodka was still liquid, he was frozen solid. His mother stopped hearing music after that and although they never forgot his father, they grew used to being two. Sometimes, when he had a bad dream he would creep into bed beside her. Sometimes he would wake in the morning to find his mother in his bed, her long eyes closed and her thin white arms all wrapped around him.

But she began to sleep less and less. He didn't know why. One day she collapsed at the factory and was taken to the local hospital. The doctors gave her pills and performed operations but she did not get better. She died a week before his twelfth birthday. Constantin was not the only one. Lots of children lost parents who worked in the factory. A year later, he heard, it was closed down.

He lived by himself for a few months and waited for the authorities to send him to an orphanage. For some reason, they never did. Eventually, he was so hungry that he used to go and rifle through dustbins. One day, a man called Vladi approached him and bought him some soup in a restaurant. After a pudding of pancakes and jam, he asked him if he wanted to work at his circus. Constantin agreed.

The next day he waited with his suitcase outside the man's cheap hotel. It was then that he understood what Vladi was doing in Nadym. He invited Constantin to climb into an old green van and they drove out into the forests, along pitted tracks where birds sung unseen in thick branches. In his lap he carried a gun. After driving for hours, he stopped and examined the snow. Then he climbed out and together they followed the footprints of a female bear and her baby. They walked for several miles in the snow, and then Vladi told him suddenly to be quiet. In front of them were the bears. They looked as if they had never seen people before and didn't run away. Vladi shot the mother with one sharp crack. He snatched the baby bear from the red snow and handed her to Constantin.

"She is yours," Vladi told him. "You must teach her to dance."

On the way back to the town, Constantin looked at the little bear with its sharp little claws and big teeth and was frightened. The little bear looked at him with his big winter boots and his father's gloves and was frightened too. He called her Nina.

The circus was not a good circus. They stopped in town squares or wide city parks, cleared the space of pigeons and performed their show before the authorities had a chance to stop them. Vladi, dressed up in a clown costume and big shoes, did a Charlie Chaplin routine with a sick tiger. A fat lady called Nadia ate fire and showed her panties and then there was Constantin, a boy who sang a right handed tune and danced with a bear. And after every show, it was always the same scenario; not enough food and Vladi so drunk on the takings that he grew violent towards Nadia. At night, Constantin would curl up to sleep beside his bear and wonder how long they would have to endure such a life.

"In the cold, cold north, you can forget as easily as the winter storm makes you forget the trees in the distance," he told me. "But as we travelled, I became like spring and I thawed a little. I grew sad when I made Nina dance for men with heads thick with vodka and felt bad for the tiger that wanted to doze all day and could not be angry."

Russia is a poor country and Vladi was not happy with the money they collected. And so they performed for longer and drove all night to cover more territory. In the town of Luza, he beat the tiger until it died. Nadia wanted to leave but Vladi would not let her. Three weeks later he found her hanging from a tree, her large fat body dangling like a doll.

After that, Vladi became scared. He believed that the police were chasing him and stopped performing himself. In the evenings he sent Constantin and Nina out dancing and demanded they bring him back the money. And every night he spent it all on vodka which he drank as he drove to the next town. Only the few kopecks Constantin could pocket without Vladi noticing kept them both from starving.

One day in summer, they crossed a border and entered Poland. They drove until they reached the town of Krakow. The next day Vladi sent them out again but the people stared at his torn clothes and worn out Siberian boots. They were shocked by Nina's mangy fur and raw skin where the metal collar had chaffed her neck.

And Constantin realised that the people gave them money not because they were amused by his dance with the bear but because they felt sorry for them.

The centre of Krakow was a place where dozens of people entertained or sold things. It is a beautiful medieval square with a clock at the top of the tower, arches below and smooth, polished cobbles. Constantin remembered that on the day they arrived there were stalls selling puppets and hats, honey and almonds, and beside the fountain, an old man with a huge bag made out of carpet was sitting on a blanket. After they had danced, Vladi chained Nina to a metal fence, took the key and left Constantin with enough money for a loaf of bread. And so they sat there in the shade for the rest of the day and waited.

The old man with the carpetbag was not from Poland or Russia. People crowded around him eager to buy little bottles of liquid from inside his bag. But he wouldn't give them to all and everybody at random. First he would look at the buyer, feel their skin, examine their tongues and then shout out one of four things.

"A weebitty too much air, a weebitty too much water, heavens above what fire, and earthy, by golly too earthy."

"I knew he was aware that I was watching him and I noticed that he looked nervous-sideways at Nina," Constantin told me. "The day grew old and Vladi did not return. As the bells in the church struck ten, the streets suddenly became quiet and I watched as the old man packed up. He wore the strangest clothes, a brightly coloured skirt and long thick woollen socks with little green ribbons at the top. And his face was like broken stone with eyes as blue as the sky in June. Eventually, he looked at me, his mouth smile-wrinkly, and spoke.

"You'll be wanting tae share my piece?" the old man said.

He held out a loaf of bread, a large salami and a bottle of orange liquid. I was mad-hungry by then and thought he wanted me to dance. Nina growled a little as I roused her up then our feet went paddy paddy on the polished square and my voice rose up in the air like steam. When we had finished, he clapped and shook his head.

"Ye didnae need tae," he said. "I didnae ask ye to dance for your supper."

And then he patted the blanket beside him, and shared his food with the boy and the bear. That is how Constantin first met Magnus.

That night Magnus bought them both from Vladi for the price of a bottle of vodka. But the next day Vladi was furious. He shouted that he had been cheated, fooled by a filthy westerner in a skirt. At that time Westerners were watched sometimes and he threatened to run to the secret police and have them both arrested.

Constantin left Krakow with Magnus in Vladi's old van. Vladi drove off in Magnus' green Rover. The van broke down in the Czech town of Ostrava and was fixed up on the condition that it had to be driven very slowly. Magnus was worried about Nina and although Constantin tried to show him that she was tame, she scratched him by mistake on the face. He may have regretted what he had done, that he had bought a small bear and a boy almost by accident and so Constantin tried his best to please him, pointing to his bottles and asking in sign language what they were.

It was then that Magnus realised that Constantin may have some purpose after all. They had stopped at a small empty campsite beside the Vlatava River on the outskirts of Prague. Using the elements at hand, Magnus taught him about the four humours, about air, fire, water and earth. And then bringing out an old pestle and mortar made out of a shiny brown deer horn, he demonstrated how he cooked cures with strange blends of dried plants, powders, liquids and metals.

The next day, they chained Nina to a tree, well hidden from the road, climbed into Vladi's truck and drove into the centre of Prague. In a tiny flat on the top floor with a wide window overlooking the old Town Square, were about thirty people of all different nationalities. For the next five hours, they drank strong coffee, smoked cigarettes and talked. They were all as old as Magnus and like him, had stained, scarred fingers. One by one they took the floor to speak, or, in some cases, to light tiny flames and demonstrate bright-burning magic. Constantin had been invited into a secret circle of Europe's last remaining alchemists and was introduced as Magnus' new pupil.

It was a risky decision. But, he told him later, it was like love at first sight. He knew from the very start that Constantin would not fail him. And in many ways he was right.

It was late when they returned to the campsite. Magnus drove down the little lane and the eyes of the car ran a blank across the place where Nina should have been. The chain had been cut. Nina had been stolen.

Of course they searched for Nina and found lots of bears, bears with miserable swaying heads and patches without fur, bears with yellow teeth and sad eyes, bears who had danced for so long the soles of their feet had become encrusted with sores. They looked in zoos, circuses and travelling shows but found no trace. Nina had disappeared.

A fortnight later they seemed to have exhausted all possibilities. One morning the old green van refused to start and Magnus decided it was time to leave. They headed to the train station on foot.

"We could not search for Nina any longer," Constantin said. "Every day our chances of finding her were a little smaller. I knew this. But as we sat aboard the still waiting train, my eyes could not rest and still I searched for her. I saw only the grey dust of the city and the blind gaze of a thousand unwashed windows."

They travelled across Europe, from Prague to Calais, France. Although Constantin had no papers, Magnus hid him inside his old carpetbag where he also placed a bag of six-day-old fish. It worked without a hitch. They crossed the English Channel at nightfall and were in Edinburgh by the following evening. The next day they stood in the shadow of the Forth Road Bridge and began to hitchhike. Together they sat in the back of post vans and tractors and looked out at the mountains and green hills. Magnus suddenly seemed to know everyone. He had been away for two years. They eventually reached a wide sound with an island: Sleat Rock.

For the first few weeks Magnus let him run loose. Constantin spent hours looking at the strange small birds with coloured beaks on the little cliffs; he picked up bright stones from the beach and explored every room of the crumbling house. And then the lessons began.

For five hours every day he read his new pupil passages from dust-thickened books. Constantin began to learn of the work of Galen, Aristotle, Paracelsus, Roger Bacon and Isaac Newton, of various ideas about the body, the spirit, the soul and the natural world. Sometimes Magnus told stories about his travels or his discoveries, which he illustrated with examples. But why, you may ask me, did Magnus still look back to disciplines that had been long discarded? Science, he would say, may have brought us the telephone, the television and nuclear power, but it has distanced us from our essence. We cannot cure all disease. We have no remedy for avarice and greed. Look to the world that made us, he would say, it will always have the answer.

But for every safe treatise in the history of alchemy, there was an equally dangerous one. The most famous of all, he taught last—the legendary Azoth, a substance that can take one material and purify it into another, making sick bodies well again or lead, gold. It is, he said, the alchemist's greatest challenge, the ultimate goal, the final test. Its creation has been attempted hundreds of times but had only been successful once or twice. The process has killed more people than it has cured.

Years passed. When he was 16, he took the oath. When he was 18, he started making his own discoveries. Many visitors came to Sleat Rock, alchemists from all over the world. They told stories of charmed snakes under the floorboards of presidents, of poisoned cocktails administered by jealous lovers and powerful aphrodisiacs slipped to movie stars by gigolos. Like Magnus, they collected stories and left remedies and recipes wherever they went for people too poor to pay doctors' bills, for sickness, unwanted babies or untreatable conditions. The remedies didn't always work. But when they did, they worked like miracles.

In the past, alchemists had sometimes travelled with circuses or fun fairs. The Masters of Matter had traversed Europe and South America for decades until they had been sacked to make way for amusement arcades or prize bingo stalls. Some of them had tried to travel on alone, performing tricks rather than creating cures and potions. But they found that few audiences wanted to be shown miraculous things anymore. They preferred to watch people risk their lives, make fools of themselves or win things. Of course, Milo Valentine knew this.

Fanny and the Masters of Matter came to Sleat Rock when they ran out of places to go. Together, at least, they thought they could stand their ground. Especially if the ground happened to be a place like Sleat Rock, where nobody ever came. And then one night, quite by chance, someone had mentioned a dancing bear, a bear with a sweet nature and large sad eyes, a bear who could understand Russian. That was how Constantin discovered what had become of Nina.

He left Sleat Rock the next day, travelled south and followed the signs until he found Valentine's. There, he was hired immediately as a flyer hander-outer and elephant keeper. After a week's work, drawn out to avoid suspicion, he discovered where her cage was and crept in during the dead of night.

"We didn't recognise each other at first," he said. "For one moment, I thought I had made a mistake. Both of us had grown tall and thin and she had a new habit of growling and showing a sharp row of yellow teeth. But when she caught my smell on the wind, she stood on her hind legs and walked slowly towards me with her head on one side and I knew it was her indeed."

It was not hard to steal her back. One night when the keeper was busy with his performance, Constantin loosened the bolts of her cage, stole her back and, in a car and trailer borrowed from Mr Air, drove all night to reach the island by the early morning. He knew no one would find her on Sleat Rock.

But the circus gave him an idea. He had spent ten years learn-ing the principles of alchemy but he needed to test them out, to go out into the world and like the great Paracelsus, collect new cures. Plus, since no one had earned any money for a considerable time and Magnus had sold off the last of his family heirlooms, he calculated that they only had enough money to last until the New Year.

And so, after many arguments and much discussion, Constantin succeeded in persuading Magnus. The Masters of Matter would perform again under the banner of a brand new circus, the Ursa Major.

At this point, Constantin paused.

"You know the rest," he said. "We failed and returned here. And then you came."

Outside it was almost dawn, soft green light spreading from the east into another day, which no matter what happened, could never be quite the same as the day before. Constantin stood up. And I swear he seemed to have shrunk several inches. There seemed to be less of him, like he was blurred around the edges.

Then we both heard something; a whirring sound, a motor echoing off the sheer rock, a boat approaching. He rushed to the window and then headed towards the stairs.

"Wait here," he said.

Minutes later he was back. His face was pinched hard and pale.

"We must hide," he said. "There are men coming. Men with guns. They must have seen the smoke from the fire."

Behind a door on the lower floor, there was a monk's bolthole in the old stone slabs. Constantin wrenched it open and the smell of mould and damp rose up to greet us in a great fug. He carried Magnus down a few steps and laid him on the red bedspread on the rough earth below. It was almost pitch black in there apart from a pale, hazy light filtering down from a small window at ground level. I ducked down too, and he pulled the bolthole cover back into its place.

Outside, the sound of the motor suddenly cut out. The boat had landed on the island. We crouched in the dark and listened. I could hear voices approaching the house, but could only make out the murmur of words, not the meaning.

The men must have stood and looked at the burning mansion for some time before they saw her. And then they started to shout and their tone changed. I thought about the boys in the cars and the way I had scared them off in Constantin's bear suit. I was partly to blame. We heard them spread out, we heard them shouting with excitement, and then we heard the crack and echo of a volley of bullets. In the underwater light of our hiding place, Constantin's face froze.

It was noon when we finally ventured out. Magnus' sleep was so deep that he barely made a murmur as he was laid back on the bed on the upper floor again. The men had gone. Constantin put on his coat and headed out without saying a word.

A few minutes later, Magnus woke with a start. He sat up, looked at me and something in his eyes made it clear that he knew that I knew everything.

"Helena," he said, using my name for the first time. "I have something to tell you."

And then he beckoned me over and whispered something in my ear. When Constantin came back ten minutes later, Magnus had already been dead for five. He had simply lain back, sighed loudly and stopped breathing. Much later, as we buried his body, I cried. But it was not only for Magnus and the bear, but for us.

I flip the manuscript shut. Life is slow to focus. Too full of words, you see. I make myself some breakfast, cereal, dry, no milk; no tea-bags left either.

I try and eat a bowl of Crunchy Nutty Flakes but they seem too noisy in my mouth. I put down the spoon with a small clank. Now there's silence. My silence, not the pseudo silence of the city, which is still full of noise, silence in my own few feet of space. Everything still looks the same; my window sees the way birds do, my rings that hang-sway so gently, my book of lonely hearts, my rooms at the top. But it's me. I miss the sound of a voice I can't even remember ever hearing.

The phone rings and makes me jump. And suddenly, unwittingly, I have this irrational certainty, this foolish confidence, just for a flash, that it will be her on the other end. Her, calling from a phone box from the mainland of her story. Her standing enclosed in a red box with Constantin the bear man waiting outside. Her listening to the shrill tone as it echoes in my here and now.

"Hello," I say with a voice, which comes out accidentally low.

There is a pause, an intake of breath and my heart leaps. It is. It is. It is.

Not. I am going mad.

"Is that the veterinary surgeon?" says a worried old man on the other end.

My mouth is suddenly so dry that I can't speak. I wish, I wish, I wished. I wished so much my hand almost crushes the receiver.

"No," I whisper. "Wrong number."

The man hangs up with a sniff and I see him perched in a flat like mine with a sick budgie lying motionless on the sawdust of its cage.

I wonder. I wonder how stupid I must have been to put my faith in a piece of plastic covered with buttons. Stupid when I know that her heart stopped like a clock and she has been dead for most of my life, dead for seventeen years. Dead. A word that comes out like a full stop. A word that feels shrouded with the hard shells of four letters. You can say it fine but its echo catches at the back of your throat like a smell. Not like passed on: a traffic offence. Deceased: a kind of scientific process. Condoled: a new sport. I prefer late. As if they are just about to arrive. As if they haven't gone too far. Maybe, I imagine, she has positioned two mirrors and has just disappeared for a time, maybe she has found herself stuck between prisms of light and glass, and maybe she is still whole and alive and here. But I know that's just rank, dumb, foolhardy sentimentality. And so I pinch myself, hard, just to make myself feel made of skin and nerves and bone and blood again.

Outside the motorway and the industrial estate look grey and flat. I want to believe in heaven but it's so hard when everything gets demolished, closes down or disappears one day in a box.

I lie and listen for the sound of the post. When it comes, it slips through the letterbox and barely makes a sound as it hits the floor. One letter. Addressed to the Occupier.

It is to happen in two days time. I am being issued, the letter says, a final demand to vacate the premises. In bold lettering at the bottom I am reminded that force will be used if necessary for my own safety. Is that an oxymoron? I think it is. I always knew that the council was staffed by morons. Take Julie, for example.

What am I to do? I look out of my flying bird-high window. Tomorrow, I decide to decide. Tomorrow.

Act III

Disappearing Act

Chapter ten
Night of the Nines

J uliet de Bleu was four feet tall. Constantin and I first met her on the shortest night of the year at the height of the short Scottish summer. The sky didn't reach pitch black, it just dimmed a little, as if yesterday was too glorious to let go and was allowed, just once, to spill into tomorrow.

Although Juliet seemed old, she wore pink lipstick, a short slip and high-heeled sandals. She had been cured of something fatal as a child at Lourdes and her much younger illuminated face with a beatific smile upon it lit up many a French mantelpiece. I remember she smelled of stale biscuits, Parma violets and talcum powder. But Juliet was beautiful in the same way that arthritic Siamese cats can be beautiful. There was something extraordinary about the shape of her head, her long thin neck and the clarity of her large grey eyes. And there was something miraculous about her presence. In fact, Juliet de Bleu had foiled certain death more than once.

Constantin and I had left Sleat Rock three months previously. And already the night where we had rowed across the sound seemed an age away. But I would never forget the oars as they slipped into

the water, turning the sea to treacle, and the way that Constantin
held my hand as I climbed out so firmly that I realised he needed
me more than he could have ever admitted. Somewhere, the tables
had turned, you see.

I withdrew all my savings from a bank in Fort William. If we were
frugal, I had calculated we had enough money to last until Christmas. And then, I figured, a plan of action would become apparent.

We had taken Magnus' car but we lived in the most meagre
of accommodations, for few landlords were willing to rent out even
the dingiest rooms to a couple like us. A winter on the island had
made us both look like vagrants. And so we camped out in rooms
with peeling wallpaper and no hot water until we couldn't bear them
any longer or someone more respectable came along.

You might think that my luck had taken a turn for the worse,
but you would be wrong. The loss of the alchemists and of Nina, the
dancing bear, had a surprising effect. The proximity of death to life,
the realisation that it runs below us like a long dark river, threatening
to swallow us up when we least expect it, changed me. And it changed
him. I can only explain it as a kind of waking. Extraordinary things
began to happen to us, maybe I now see, because we let them.

What do I mean? Well, to give you just one example, complete strangers would invite us to their weddings (it happened three
times and once Constantin was even asked to give away the bride).
I think it was because we seemed so deliriously alive. The world had
invited us to stay a little longer and we were glad.

It was two in the morning on midsummer night when we
drove along Princes Street in Magnus' barely roadworthy Morris
Minor. Edinburgh is a place used to rain, to a cold east wind and
seeping dampness, so balmy weather always took people by surprise.
The houses weren't built with any meteorological optimism; windows didn't open properly, carpets and thick rugs were suffocational
and nobody could sleep without the weight of blankets.

Adults stood rubbing their eyes on their ornamental balconies or behind their inoperative windows, looking over the city and trying to make sense of the numbers on their clocks. Children sneaked out in their pyjamas to play with the hoses which watered the shrubs in the council's flower beds, while teenagers met up to drink cider in parks which had long since bolted their gates.

On the main road, despite the hour, traffic streaked past us relentlessly. Lots of strange things sped through the city without anyone ever knowing, and that night there was a convoy of large lorries and animal trailers. It was a circus menagerie, one that had been bought in its entirety from a circus near Paris. In a line of thirty trailers were the usual elephants, horses, camels and dogs. But there were also llamas, peacocks, birds of paradise and a giraffe.

But we were unaware of all this then. The lights changed and Constantin fumbled with the gears. Pushing the stick into third instead of first, he slammed his foot on the clutch and stalled the car. A lorry ploughed into our bumper with an explosion of glass and metal. Behind us we heard a series of smashes and bumps, an aural domino run. But the skid of tyres and the hiss of engines were underlined by other sounds. The unmistakable noise of a stampede, the flap and gallop of two dozen exotic animals as they escaped from their boxes and cantered, padded, or flew off into the night.

We climbed out. Right behind us was a spectacular vista of four-wheeled devastation. The piled-up convoy stretched in a nose to tail line and snaked back along the road for almost quarter of a mile. Luckily, it was soon clear that there were no serious injuries, just vehicle damage. Half a dozen drivers were standing by the roadside shouting at each other or scratching their heads. In the distance a dog barked. The air around was milky dark. As I listened I could hear the crash and thump of several more cars as they ploughed into the back of the line. In the houses beside the road, lights came on one by one and local residents in their dressing gowns started to cluster in doorways.

"Heavens above!" Constantin exclaimed. "What happened?"

I looked at him across the roof of our now undriveable car and felt a wave of relief that he was safe and there and with me.

Just at that moment, however, a voice rang out from behind me.

"Stop right there!"

Juliet de Bleu strode towards us along the middle of the road. And as she approached, I heard a noise, a low growl, a dim rumble; the woman was humming under her breath. At first I thought it was an unconscious vocal tick as she planned what to say next. But now I'm not so sure. It was a sort of vocal drum roll, an articulated pause, a reverberating semi-colon that made you stop talking and pay attention.

"Is this," she said eventually, looking down her long thin nose at our wrecked vehicles, "yours?"

Constantin nodded and then looked at me for help.

"In a manner of speaking," I replied. The woman started to hum and we waited for her next words with increasing trepidation.

"Do you know what you have done?" she said eventually, her voice alternating between a girlish lilt and a cigarette croak "You have written off the entire convoy."

"I'm very sorry," said Constantin. "My deepest apologies."

"Never mind," she said. "Your insurance will have to pay. To whom shall I make out the claim?"

We glanced at each other. Juliet noticed.

"You do have insurance?" she asked.

A cold wave swept right through me. Constantin blanched.

"A license, tax... an M.O.T.?"

"We'll pay you back," Constantin said. "How much?"

Juliet hummed louder. Constantin pulled out his wallet; a wallet I knew was practically empty.

"Don't," I shouted. They both turned and looked at me. I opened my mouth but this time nothing came out. I cleared my throat.

"Don't call the police."

You see, I suddenly suspected that I was about to lose him again. A minor traffic offence would lead to a dock, a sentence, and a deportation order, for, despite the fact that he had been living in

Scotland for years, Magnus hadn't bothered, as a matter of principle, with paperwork. Constantin had never been naturalized, he was never legal. Since we had left Sleat Rock, Constantin hadn't mentioned his former vocation. It seemed as though he had cut that part of his life adrift, let it go. It seemed as though he had chosen me. And now that the odds that he would be stolen away by alchemy were lengthening, he was about to be snatched away by something altogether more mundane.

Juliet took a packet of filter-less cigarettes from her handbag and placed one in her mouth. She paused for a fraction of a second. Acting on cue, Constantin pulled a box of matches from his pocket and struck one. The night was still but the flame leapt in the breeze, burning his finger. He tossed the match into the other hand and clutched it in his fist until only a small green flame was visible. She stared at it. Her humming stopped. Constantin smiled, touched it with his finger and it burned lilac.

Juliet de Bleu looked from one of our faces to the other and then at the car. She let out a throaty laugh.

"How do you do that?"

Constantin shrugged.

She leaned over the flame and sucked until the end of her cigarette burned red.

"Never mind," she said blowing smoke through her nose. "He can afford it."

Before I go further, I must explain Juliet de Bleu. We had accidentally bumped into a woman who you could sometimes spot in the background of photographs of celebrities at restaurant openings. Behind film stars and minor European royalty, you could often make out her shoulder or her hand clutching a glass of champagne. At that point she was employed by one of Britain's richest Pop Stars; her job, to produce a steady supply of sensational acts to amuse him and his friends. The ménage of animals had followed a successful run of human freaks, including the world's smallest lady and the man with three eyes.

"Are you working?" she asked us both.

"Not at the moment," I replied.

"I organize parties, very exclusive, only the top acts. I like the look of you," she said to Constantin. She opened her handbag and pulled out a business card. As well as her name, there were half a dozen telephone numbers already scored out. With a pencil, she wrote another number in curly handwriting.

"Call this number," she said, "and tell them that you were told to by Juliet de Bleu. "They are always looking for attractive bar staff."

And with that she strode off again, her spindly figure thrown into sharp relief by the approach of half a dozen emergency vehicles.

Constantin tore the card in two and shoved the pieces deep into his pocket. And then he walked round the car and took my hand.

"Come on," he said. "Let's go."

In half-glow of dawn, with the shuttered up shops and a sky busy with stars, the city felt unfamiliar, foreign. Two little boys cantered down Hanover Street on the back of a zebra. An elephant was holding a hose in its trunk, a curve of shiny water splashing on to the grey pavement where a group of children shrieked with delight. And even the emergency services with their flashing lights and wailing sirens added to the general feeling of otherness. As drivers and policemen chased animals, birds and children, there was a sense of spontaneous carnival, of hilarious festival as beasts and humans, all tired of being cooped up in trucks or houses that were too small, ran wild together in the midsummer night.

The gate had been left open to Princes Street Gardens. No one saw us enter, no one saw us lie down on the soft moss beneath a cherry tree. When a gust caught its branches, a shower of late blossoms fell, covering us in white.

Hours later, when most of the animals had been rounded up, only remnants such as a brightly coloured feather in a drain or a huge pile of dung on a zebra crossing could convince people that they had not been dreaming. But it did take five firemen two days to coax a monkey down from a water tower and a week for the council to clear up all the mess. Some of the animals were never retrieved. A llama, two poodles and a peacock disappeared completely. A zebra turned up months later in excellent health, after being looked after in a derelict greenhouse by three local school children, who managed to feed it using their school dinner money.

I remember the weight of Constantin's arm across my belly. I remember his slow breath on my neck. I remember watching him wake and the way he looked at me as if there, in my arms under a luminous sky, was the one place he knew he belonged. If my story had only ended here, what a story it would have been.

Later that day we spotted an advertisement for a housekeeper placed by an elderly gentleman in Musselburgh. We moved into the basement flat of a house in a smart terrace after I had impressed Captain Morrison with my general knowledge. He too was a scholar of the Encyclopaedia Britannica but had only reached the fourth volume. He may have been an expert on fly fishing, but bowed to my superior grasp of the geography and history of Hadrian's Wall.

Anyway, my duties were light, since the Captain didn't like to be disturbed. I hoovered once a week to coincide with the Captain's night at his club in town, and tiptoed round the house every morning while he was still asleep dusting his golf trophies and washing his dishes.

If Constantin was still haunted by what had happened on Sleat Rock, he seldom showed it. He learned to cook and took great pleasure in making his own bread and baking cakes. As well as cooking supper every night, he brought me breakfast in bed. One morning I woke to find the whole room full of wild flowers. Huge heads of cow parsley, dandelions and pink campion stood in jam jars on the window ledge. Bees, bugs and grasshoppers, which he had inadvertently brought in too, dropped from their leaves and lazily buzzed around the room.

One day he laid a dress on my bed. Underneath panels of hand-stitched gauze, he had placed translucent green lime leaves. I put it on and rustled softly. One night he brought me a rare butterfly in a jar. The colours on its wings were brighter than paint and drawn with a finer point than you could ever use. Nobody could have given me more precious gifts. They were all the proof I needed.

And yet they were also evidence of another truth, if only I had seen it. Everything was dead within hours, the flowers with fallen heads, the leaves turned brown, and the butterfly a corner of brown paper at the bottom of the jar. And sometimes in the middle of night I would wake to hear him talking in his sleep.

"Stage Four already... you haven't lost the acid... turn down the heat before the glass cracks..."

Occasionally, he would wake with a start and his hand would grip my arm.

"Magnus?" he would say.

"No," I would reply. "It's me. Helena."

And then he would remember where he was and with whom. He could not go back. Magnus was dead. He had broken his oaths. And so he would lie awake, waiting for morning, waiting for me to stir.

It was soon obvious, however, that Constantin needed something to do. Since his options were limited, he picked raspberries for three weeks on a local farm and then helped with the potato crop.

"What do you think about when you work?" I asked him.

"Sometimes nothing," he replied. "Sometimes you."

I don't know whose idea it was that he become a children's conjuror. It may have been suggested by a book he found which belonged to the Captain called *The A–Z of Magic*. I bought him a black opera cape from a charity shop and handwrote a dozen posters that we put in shop windows.

His only competitor was Kevin the Magnificent, a bad tempered ex-vicar in his fifties, who didn't like children. His delivery may have been professional but Kevin's tricks were badly homemade and involved copious secret compartments into which things "vanished." All but the dimmest of five-year olds could figure out how his tricks worked but most were too scared to say.

Constantin was hired on the condition that he didn't frighten the children. He was an instant success. Remember this was a man who enjoyed exploding fruit. His act was fast and funny and when the children guessed how a trick was done, he took great pleasure in revealing that they were quite wrong. Occasionally he accidentally set a paper lampshade on fire or made a child disappear and forgot about them, but nobody ever complained. The children were always located sooner or later, usually by their banging.

When he was particularly busy, we lived almost exclusively on children's party food. Mothers, harassed to the point of madness, filled our pockets with birthday cake and chipolata sausages. They thrust coloured napkins filled with chocolate biscuits and egg sandwiches into our hands and wouldn't let us leave unless we had eaten our fill of jelly and ice cream. They were grateful, you see, grateful for an hour of peace in an afternoon of mayhem. Because Constantin had a way with children. He could make them listen to him, he could make them sit still, and he could make them believe almost anything.

The girl's name was Hesterella McNaughton. I remember her quite clearly, probably because she was wearing a yellow dress not unlike the ones from the missionary bible class that my mother used to make me wear. Her mother dropped her off an hour too early, having lost the invitation with the time the party started on it, and when we arrived, she was sitting all alone in the corner of the garden absent-mindedly pulling all the petals from a begonia bush. It said in the papers that she had just turned eight but to me she looked much younger.

Part of Constantin's act involved throwing a load of disgusting ingredients into a hat to make a birthday cake. That afternoon he invited Hesterella to help him and one by one she chucked tubs of shoe polish, toothpaste, black pepper and washing up liquid into a large black Fedora he had bought for the purpose in the Grassmarket. And then with a green flash, he produced a chocolate and hazelnut cake, which he had made earlier from a recipe in a Sunday newspaper.

The birthday child, a ruddy-faced boy wearing a cowboy outfit, was invited to cut a slice and eat it. Delicious, he proclaimed. Constantin took a bow and asked his helper to do the same. As thirty children applauded, he offered a piece of cake to Hesterella. She hesitated. Constantin urged her to try it. Later, he said he thought she thought it was still made of toothpaste and boot polish, of black pepper and washing up liquid. He said he just wanted to show her that the magic had worked.

"Go on," he said. "Eat. It won't poison you, I promise."

Hesterella's left hand clenched the hem of her dress while her right reached out to the plate. With a small grimace, she picked up a slice. Then she opened her mouth and closed her eyes tight shut. As soon as her lips closed on the cake, however, they started to swell.

By this time, Constantin had begun his next trick. He was throwing coloured handkerchiefs into the birthday boy's pocket. He didn't notice what was happening until the room went dead silent. Then he looked up and realised that the children weren't mesmerised by the trick but by the sight of Hesterella McNaughton's lips. Like two raw pork sausages, they had doubled in size. Her face was the colour of watered down milk and her eyes were so dilated they looked like a couple of chocolate buttons. Her hand reached up to her throat as she struggled for breath.

"Excuse me," she said, "excuse me…"

Just at that moment, the birthday boy's mother breezed in trailing the faint whiff of a recently downed gin. The smile on her face faded as she took in what had happened. With a shout, she pounced on Hesterella and shook the slice of cake from her hand. Then she tried to prise her mouth open and remove any cake she could see.

"Call an ambulance," she yelled.

Constantin was rooted to the spot. He looked at the cake. He tasted it. He didn't understand.

"Didn't she tell you," the mother said as Hesterella's face turned blue, "she's allergic to nuts."

As we waited for the ambulance, Constantin stared at his hands. I knew what he was thinking. But there was nothing he could do. Nothing.

Some people blamed the mother, others, Mrs McNaughton, a woman so absent-minded that she had forgotten as usual to include Hesterella's emergency syringe of adrenalin in her sequined party handbag. But as poor little Hesterella McNaughton lay in the intensive care unit of the Royal Infirmary, most took some kind of morbid pleasure in reporting how the children's conjuror had almost forced the cake down the girl's throat.

Bookings dropped off rather sharply after that.

My little girl, did I already tell you that you were positioned the wrong way in my womb, your backbone to my backbone, your face looking out instead of in. You were born facing the night sky, your head was blue, as it was quite a struggle for both of us, and on your face was a look of steely determination. When you opened your eyes and looked at me, the midwife said, by golly, she's been here before. But in truth, you were nearly never here at all.

As I have already written, alchemists must swear to secrecy and celibacy. They had much to conceal, much to hide. Anything or anybody that swayed the mind or weakened the will could not be tolerated. Lovers were absolutely forbidden—as well as the risk of leakage, there was always the chance that an accident might happen.

"Of all the things that might befall you, fathering a child is the worst," Magnus had told Constantin, "you might as well kill yourself."

It was easy to see why. A child would stretch their loyalty to the limit, a child would change their priorities, and a child would weaken their resolve.

"Nothing will work the way it should," Magnus continued, "Your touch, lost; your mind, fragmented. All our learning gathered over thousands of years and passed down to you will be rendered meaningless in one stroke. It will leave you impotent and broken. You cannot let it happen."

All alchemists knew how to cause a miscarriage. As well as a cure for the common cold, it was one of their most requested potions. And yet, despite all this, I really believed that there was no going back, no turning tables; it was far too late for that. Anyhow, by this point, Constantin's oaths were well and truly broken.

After the cake incident, Constantin barely slept at all, as if by force of will he could stretch and stretch and then pull himself back, as if he could elasticate time. Then, one morning he rose early and came back at lunchtime with a large plastic bag. Inside was a second hand fur coat, long and black and made of bear. He put it on, curled up and went to sleep. Hesterella was dead.

"I think we need to talk," I said, which was stating the obvious.

"If you like," he said.

It must have been late September then. The leaves on the trees had started to turn and filled the air with their crisp orange and yellow. We put on our coats and walked down beside the Water of Leith. Blackberries dropped in clusters from bramble bushes and the path was muddy underfoot.

We walked up some wooden steps and on to a bridge. With one leap, he jumped on the stone ledge, high above the water.

"What are you doing?" I said. "Please be careful."

But he kept on walking, one foot in front of the other along the slippery moss-covered wall. And then he turned and looked down at me.

"I promised her," he said.

"What are you talking about?" I replied.

"I am no good," he replied. "I lied."

Something inside me snapped. It wasn't his fault. He didn't know. But he had to stop blaming himself.

"Well go on," I said. "Jump if you feel that bad."

He turned. He placed his feet on the edge. I panicked; I leapt up on to the parapet.

"No," I shouted, "I didn't mean it,"

He turned in surprise, he lost his balance. But just before he toppled I grabbed him with both arms. And so we both fell over the edge. But we did not fall into the Water of Leith. My weight had pushed us to the left and instead we fell straight through the branches of an elderflower bush before crashing into the soft decaying undergrowth below.

I remember the touch of bear fur against my cheek. I was back in the Eiffel years before. At first I wondered if I was dead. But I could feel my warm breath in the cold air and the smell of mothballs caught in my throat. And then I wondered if he was dead. I looked up and saw his face. He was staring up through the trees, his eyes the colour of rain.

"Is anything broken?" I asked. But he did not answer.

A bone, a heart, an oath; once something is broken, can it be fixed as if it were never broken at all? And once something is there, is almost visible to the human eye, can you just wipe it away and pretend it never existed? As the Water of Leith flowed down to the Forth below us, I shouted, I wailed, I wept, I refused. The man I loved was an alchemist. He was not like other people. He believed that the Azoth could cure people from all illness and pain, he believed it could change the nature of things, he believed in miracles. All he had to do was make it.

The air crackled with the smell of wood smoke. He drew me close and whispered into my hair.

"You're the only one," he said.

But his words had two meanings. Maybe I was the only one he loved or maybe I was the only one who knew.

Prrrrrrring. The doorbell. Prrrrrring. It's late. Too late for workmen. Too late for Julie. The ropes creak, the leather rings sigh as I approach the door. The fisheye is glazed white with the colour of the hall walls under the strip light. The door's locked now. Not in case of burglars ohhhnono. They can't get past the man at the gate with the dog.

I look through the hole. A Russian hat and lowered eyes. It's you; you, curved so your mouth stretches tight across your face like a red bandage, you with tiny cartoon feet and minuscule shoes. You look up, quite quickly and one eye approaches, one huge eye of blue flecked with green. Before the eye can gulp me up or bowl me over like a great big marble, you pull away again. And then I hear your feet clump clump clump, clump clump clump tic tic on the stairs.

I watch your window. See your light. For once the blinds are drawn. I should have opened the door; you should have waited. I lie awake forever. I sleep. Sleep. Doze. Sleep. Dream a little. Forget. Sleep. Remember. Wake. Then BANG. I sit up. BANG, CRACK. SCCREEK. It takes me several seconds to work out what the noise is and where forheavenssake it's coming from. And then I see a blunt shark-nose metal point, sticking through the wood. SCCREEK, it is pulled out again. An axe is trying to break down my door.

There is nowhere to hide. Nowhere I wouldn't be found. I wonder if I could swing from the balcony in some sort of James Bondian manoeuvre but it's much too high. I cover my ears to drown out the terrible noise, the sound of a wooden door screaming as it is split right down its painted middle. Stop whirring stupid mind.

The built-in oven is far too small. Far Too Small. To the regular sound of the swing of the axe, I fold myself in, leg after leg, shoulder after shoulder and arm after arm. They are almost inside. I can tell by the slackness of the stroke. I grab the manuscript, fold in my head and pull the door to. I thought it would be blackascoal in here. But there is a thin shaft of light from the crack of the door.

They are searching for me. Doors swing, seats creak as they look beneath them, my letters crisp in their dirty workman's hands, nosy buggers. When they think I am long gone, they relax. One puts the kettle on and they brew themselves a cup of tea. What bloody cheek, what bloody, bloody cheek. My eyes spit tears.

"We'll have to clear this lot," one of them says.

"I know," says the other. "There's always one."

One what? I think. One cabbage. One stupid hermit who

won't leave. One of me in every block across the land. Or one of you.

They start to move my stuff. My green mountain-colour sofa, my table, my chairs, and my teapot. Some of it they seem to be putting in boxes. Some of it they throw out of the window. I hear their exertion and then start counting: one two three four five… before a loud crash from below. I don't care. No, I don't care.

It is just about light enough to read. Like an origami girl I have folded almost square. I can just about turn the pages. I read. I need the answers. I need to know. What happened next? And the other question, the obvious one.

Chapter eleven

Alchemy

I t was around this time that I began to hear the explosions again. At night the crack of detonation and the low boom of impact would wake me, rattling the windows and shaking the furniture. When I opened my eyes, however, our room was always still. The only movement would be a breath of night air on our curtains and the faintest prickle of the stars. Constantin was rarely beside me. I would climb out of bed and pad softly to the living room. And there he would be, dozing awkwardly beneath his bear coat on the sofa, or sitting with his palms facing upwards in the dark, wide awake.

It was I who called Juliet. I riffled through Constantin's pocket until I found the torn strips of her business card. I called her because I couldn't bear it any longer. I called her because I suspected that despite his assurances to the contrary, I knew I simply wasn't enough.

This makes him sound callous and uncaring, but it wasn't true. Guilt blasts holes inside people and makes them hollow. Constantin's body had become simply a costume he wore. He was fading from the inside out. I had to do something.

Juliet didn't remember me. She said she vaguely remembered Constantin. And she was short with me, short and abrupt and in the middle of a meeting. I nearly hung up; I nearly slammed down the phone in a fit of temper. But I took a deep breath and told her. Her meeting seemed to dissipate like ether.

"An alchemist," she said in a whisper. "Can you give me any evidence of this?"

"No," I said. "You'll have to come and see for yourself."

Of course, Constantin refused. He pointed out that he could not practice. His oaths were broken. He had no books, no equipment.

"One performance only," I pleaded. "You make enough money to set yourself up again. And then whompf, you disappear."

"Alchemy is not entertainment," Constantin replied. "I have learned that already."

"You want to help people?" I insisted. "To cure the sick with remedies from nature? How can you do that by sitting here all day?"

"I said no," he said. But I saw that his resolve was weakening. I knew it would.

"For Hesterella, then," I whispered.

Constantin paused. He stared out of the window and his eyes seemed to soak up the blackness of the glass. And then something within him snapped. He stretched, inhaled and filled himself with the morning.

"I'll think about it," he said.

I kissed him on his cool smooth cheek. I told him it was the right thing to do. But deep inside my chest the gelignite cracked once more.

You see, I'll tell you what Magnus told me on Sleat Island. His long thin fingers grabbed my arm and he pulled me towards him until my ear was close to the tremble of his mouth. His deep voice had lost its motor and sometimes ground to a halt in mid-sentence. But still he struggled to continue. And this is what he said; that

Constantin would never belong to me; his body might betray his heart, but not for long.

These I could take as the ranting of a jealous mind, the last outpourings of love for an adopted son who he was about to lose. No, I could fight these. It was his last pronouncement that shook me most deeply.

"You must stop him making the Azoth."

"Why?" I said, "Tell me why?"

"Can't you see?" he replied. "It will destroy him, just as it destroyed us."

"You made it?"

Magnus nodded, his scored cheeks forming deep crevasses for his tears to run down. And then he just sighed deeply, closed his eyes and was suddenly still, so very still that I stared and stared at his face, waiting for something else, not quite believing that he was gone. But in minutes, his body had changed its form and he had become as inanimate as a lump of granite.

Maybe if he had never told me, I would not have done the things I did. But I misunderstood. I got it wrong.

I remember Juliet de Bleu perched on the edge of our sofa with a cup of tea on her lap. It was late autumn but her legs were bare and brown. I remember the look on her face as she watched Constantin perform for her. It was filled both with delight and regret. And when he finished, she shivered, as if her body was suddenly aware of the warmth denied her, the warmth that hitherto she had never even known existed.

"When can you start?" she said.

Constantin's face showed no expression. Even the flourish of his lips was silent and unreadable.

"Well?" Juliet said.

He paused before he spoke. But when he did, it was clear that he had banished all doubt.

"Sometimes it is necessary to compromise," he said.

"Is that a yes?" asked Juliet.

We left Captain Morrison's the next day in a taxi with Juliet de Bleu. He was sad to see us go. Of course he'd heard about Hesterella, but he blamed the mother.

"An irresponsible woman," he told me. "Once dropped her children off at school a whole week before term started. Janitor had to amuse them all day until she showed up, half an hour late of course."

"But she didn't deserve what happened to her," I pointed out. "She lost her daughter."

"Damn shame," Captain Morrison muttered. "Damn shame for all concerned."

The sun shone with a pale golden light that day. We crossed the River Forth and the water formed a slow flow of molten metal beneath us.

The Pop Star had a mansion just north of Perth. Juliet told us that he had offered us the guest flat in the stable wing, a very unusual move on his part.

"When I told him what you did," she said. "He was very excited."

"I am not promising anything," Constantin said.

"Of course not," said Juliet. "He just wants to give you everything you need. He likes to support people like you, to get involved. How much do you want?"

"A million pounds," he replied.

Juliet smiled.

"Very funny," she said.

The mansion was accessed through three sets of locked gates. It had been designed to resemble a small castle with turrets and circular towers. A television camera inspected us before a heavy wooden door carved with angels and gargoyles buzzed open. It was as if the place was staffed by ghosts.

Inside, every room was filled with antiques and works of art from antiquity. A Roman horse's head was mounted on a plinth in the hallway, the toilet was inside a medieval confessional booth and there were half a dozen gilded Russian icons on the walls.

"He is a collector," Juliet told us, "of precious things."

And then there was a small cough and we all turned to see a man hovering in the doorway.

"Nice to meet you at last," he said. "Please make yourself at home."

Since I was never allowed to listen to pop music as a child and Constantin was from Russia where western pop music was banned, neither of us had ever heard of the Pop Star. He looked rather ordinary, in fact, like the type of man whom, but for a fluke of fate, would have been a bank manager or a demonstrator of kitchen equipment. We offered our hands but he did not shake them. He did not look anyone in the eye either. Instead he stood, clutching a glass of milk, with a look of suffering on his face.

"Two things," he said. "You're not allowed to leave until after the performance and you must sign a confidentiality agreement. Nothing which happens in here gets out."

"That is very agreeable to me also," Constantin said.

The Pop Star rarely worked on music anymore. He had so much money, he didn't have to. The mansion sat all on its own on huge, well-kept grounds. There were tennis courts and a covered swimming pool that nobody ever seemed to use. The grass, the trees, the flowers were always both perfectly trimmed and immaculately blooming. Nothing was overgrown or decaying. Everything was frozen in a state of static perfection. It may sound bizarre, but there was never any weather. It was always still and dry. Sometimes it was so quiet it was as if the wind had been turned back at the wrought iron gates.

But occasionally in the middle of the night we'd be woken by a tumble of people slamming their way out of cars, women with high pitched laughs and men who would bellow like bulls. The parties never lasted for long, however. By six, the Pop Star would have had enough and his guests were dispatched whether they wanted to leave or not. They were often so angry that they drove off with a screech across the garden, leaving the black skid of their tyre marks on the green baize of his perfect lawn.

Every year the Pop Star threw a party to celebrate his birthday. And every year the guest list would get smaller and smaller since he had a pathological fear of being 'used.'

People did use him. They smashed his belongings and pocketed the ashtrays; they defaced his art works and used his vintage wine for punch. I felt sorry for him. He was always ill with something or other—indigestion, a cold, an insect bite that wouldn't heal. Looking back, despite the wealth, he was the unhappiest man I have ever met.

Constantin was given a large empty room with two stone sinks and a huge cauldron with a fire below it for heating water. It had once been the laundry. He had four weeks, exactly, to prepare for his one-off performance at the Pop Star's birthday party. And in that time he could have anything he wanted.

"I need mercury, lead and lemons," he asked Juliet.

My heart boomed. I knew that he would probably try to attempt the six stages again. I just didn't realize that he would do it so soon. For these were the three things he needed to try and create the Azoth.

"That can be arranged," she replied

I stood back and watched as he immersed himself in the task ahead, working all day and well into the night. His aim was to reach stage five beforehand and then perform the final stage and create the Azoth, or Philosopher's Stone, in front of the Pop Star and what remained of his friends. It was hugely ambitious, even by his standards and I doubted whether he would even reach the second stage. Remember, it had taken the alchemists on Sleat Rock all winter, and there were six of them.

He had to build a glass still, melt metal and keep liquids at the same temperature for hours on end. But even when he emerged red-eyed from fatigue and the smoke, his fingers cut and covered with minor burns, he was more buoyant than he had been for months.

"Are you okay?" I would ask.

He didn't have to reply. The corners of his mouth would curl and his eyes would be filled with promise.

"So-so" he would say. "So-so."

The Pop Star began to take an interest. He would knock quietly and then go into the laboratory. Lorries began to turn up with boxes, special delivery. Inside were rare plants and instruments from pharmaceutical companies, ingots of pure gold and vials of pure plant essence. Shelves were erected to hold dozens of bottles filled with liquids and powders. The single notebook that Constantin had rescued from the island was held open on a music stand.

One day the Pop Star gave Constantin a stuffed crocodile to hang on the ceiling. Apparently it had once belonged to John Dee. The Pop Star must have spent a fortune but Constantin barely noticed. It was a two-way thing, certainly at that point. Constantin never said anything to me, but the Pop Star complained less and less about his ailments. I gathered that Constantin was treating him with specially prepared remedies.

It was around this time that I began to feel a little peculiar. I avoided Constantin's lab; the smell made me nauseous. I lost my appetite for anything sweet, I gorged myself on Marmite on toast and dreamed strange dreams. But I wouldn't say it was all unpleasant. Since that night in Princes Street Gardens, it was as if I had been holding my breath. Something was going on inside me, making me look inwards instead of out. It was like an exhilarating carsickness, a nauseating thrill. It was a buzz and tickle, a wrench and thud—quite impossible to ignore. It was you.

I'm not sure exactly when it was that I realized that I had been shut out. Juliet and the Pop Star began to guard the door to the laboratory and field all my attempts at contact with Constantin. I saw him less and less. I would be fast asleep when he had finished at night and he would always rise before I woke. Juliet told me one day that a bed had been moved into the former laundry so that he could nap whenever he liked. But I wouldn't say I was worried. I had a jealously guarded secret of my own.

During his rare moments of rest, Constantin sought me out. I remember one day that he suggested we go for a walk. We dressed in warm coats and took off along the driveway. Two paces behind were the Pop Star, muffled up to the eyes in a cashmere scarf, and Juliet with bare legs and heels, huffing and puffing to keep up.

What were they scared of? That they would lose him? That I would steal him away? But he could not leave even if I had begged him to; apart from the three sets of locked gates to negotiate, he thought himself back on course, despite the obvious compromise. I can see him now, striding along a path crisp with frost. His shoulders were thrown back and his face glowed with happiness. He was whole again.

I would say that right at that moment in time I was happy too. It was as if we were floating on a glassy surface, blissfully unaware of the dangerous currents that ran below. Now I can see that we have the capacity to see only what we want to see and to ignore everything else. How else could I have let what happened happen?

The Pop Star's birthday approached and there were a few minor mishaps. One day the whole house was filled with the smell of burnt plastic, on another it was filled with yellow smoke. I could see that the Pop Star was having second thoughts when Constantin accidentally dropped a little of the mixture on the ground, creating a small explosion which shook his pictures from the walls and smashed several Ming vases. But nothing could stop Constantin once he had started. Any setback just made him work harder, made him all the more determined.

The day before his birthday, the Pop Star supervised the decoration of the main ballroom. It was hung with garlands of Mimosa and pleated silk drapes. All afternoon caterers had trooped into the kitchen with towering cakes and trays of smoked salmon. Several truckloads of champagne were unloaded into the basement. It was to be the biggest party he had ever held.

I remember the way Constantin looked that day. His face and hands were ashen.

"I've done it," he said. "I've made the white stone. I've reached the fifth stage."

He went to the sink to wash his hands. I started to tremble. I couldn't bear to look at him. I was suddenly scared of what lay ahead of us. I hadn't expected it, you see. Not so soon.

"Are you sure?" I asked. "I mean, how do you know it will work?"

"It will."

"But what if it didn't, what if it were dangerous instead of miraculous?"

Constantin turned, his face dark.

"Why do you say that?"

"Well it might be?"

His temper suddenly snapped. He turned on me and I barely recognized him.

"It is at the root of all my learning," he said, "Transmutation, the transformation of one impure substance to a pure one. If, as you suggest, it is dangerous rather than miraculous, then everything I believe in is false. My life has been a pointless exercise."

He paused.

"I want you to take the money," he said.

I didn't know what he meant at first. I didn't have a clue.

"The million pounds," he continued. "The Pop Star is writing a cheque made out to you."

The room suddenly felt cold.

"What do you mean?" I asked.

"It was a mistake... me and you... I see that now," he said softly. "Forgive me."

I turned away so he couldn't see my eyes moisten and spill over.

"I'll understand if you want to leave straight away?" he said.

"Do you want me to?"

I struggled with my breath. I didn't want him to see me cry. "No," he replied.

Right at that moment, the Pop Star bustled in and took up his position between us.

"They're coming at seven," he said. "Juliet has organized an act to kick things off and I thought that you could appear just after the cake, at say, midnight."

He noticed the frost in the atmosphere.

"What's wrong, what's happened?"

"I've changed my mind," Constantin said.

"You what?" said the Pop Star.

"No guests."

The party was cancelled.

I used to be the type of girl who would not give up. I used to be the type of girl who would risk everything. I used to be the type of girl who would leap without looking. But my chemistry had changed. I had grown cautious.

For the first time in four weeks, the weather broke. The next day, the Pop Star's birthday, rain fell in huge drops, knocking over the tulips and making large pools on the tennis courts.

A big black car drew up outside the mansion at around six. A woman climbed out of the driver's seat. She looked vaguely familiar. I watched as the passenger swung open the door. Even from above I recognized the black hair, which stuck up at an angle, and long wooden walking stick. It was Milo Valentine.

"Someone else is here," I told Constantin. "I thought it was going to be just you."

"So did I," he said.

Champagne was mandatory and served in the ballroom. Since there weren't any guests, the Pop Star had taken the unprecedented step of inviting the performers for a drink.

As I squeezed into a black sequined outfit that Juliet insisted I wear for the occasion, I almost convinced myself that they wouldn't recognize me. It had been a long time. And dozens of girls had passed through Valentine's since they had abandoned me in a field. Constantin had agreed to wear a hired tuxedo. It was too small for him and strained at the seams.

"Do I look ridiculous?" he asked.

"No," I lied. "No."

Rain was still cascading off the cupola above, creating a steady thrum that virtually drowned out the soft tinkle of a hired pianist. Of course they recognized me instantly but pretended they didn't. The booming began again in the pit of my stomach.

"Constantin is an alchemist," the Pop Star said.

Milo looked at Constantin and guffawed. Nobody moved. He began to laugh, harder and harder until he could hardly stand, until he had to support himself with his stick.

"That's a good one," he said eventually.

Constantin was oblivious. But from the corner of my eye I could see Juliet deflate ever so slightly. I could also see the Pop Star take just the smallest of paces away from us.

"And you," the Pop Star asked. "What do you do?"

"Nothing," Milo said. "It's my wife Clara who is the talented one."

Clara suddenly smiled, her face alive as a dozen mirrors. My teeth began to chatter despite the fact that it was warm in the ballroom. It was going to be worse, much worse than I had anticipated. Nobody said anything.

Clara started running her fingers down the silk curtains. She seemed to be inhaling the place, breathing in the almost limitless wealth. Her gaze ran over the crystal chandeliers and then down to the priceless Persian rugs. On the way it ran over me. To my horror it returned to me. I crossed my arms over my waist and breathed in as hard as I could. But the bump must have still been visible. Clara looked at me and a large red spot appeared on her cheek as if I had slapped her. Before I could turn away or try, all eyes were drawn involuntarily in my direction. I was pregnant. It was obvious.

"Still doing your act, Helena?" Milo was looking at me with an amused expression.

"No," I said softly.

"Shame. She was really very good," he said. "It was a pleasure to work with her."

Constantin drank his champagne back in one gulp. Juliet picked invisible pieces of lint from her shoulder. The Pop Star smiled.

"So you know each other?" he asked.

"No," said Clara.

"Yes," said Milo.

"Oh," said the Pop Star.

Juliet cleared her throat and then raised her glass.

"We seem to be forgetting what brought us here. Happy Birthday," she said. "To fame, fortune and happiness!"

We raised our glasses and drank. The Pop Star gulped air.

"Now, shall we begin?" he said.

The Pop Star sat in the middle of a row of gilded chairs in the empty ballroom. A stage had been erected at one end and a mirrored ball hung from the ceiling, throwing diamonds of cold light over the walls. Trees swayed outside in the rain like seaweed. It was as if the room had sunk to the bottom of the sea.

"I'm sorry, I'm sorry, I'm sorry," I whispered. "I was going to tell you. I just didn't know how."

We stood in a small anteroom that was to have held the coats. Constantin's face was taut and he was breathing too fast.

"Does it really matter?"

He looked at me and I could see my reflection in his eyes. I was suddenly small.

"Yes," he said. "I must cancel. Nothing will work, my touch lost, mind fragmented. I cannot have a child."

Juliet de Bleu walked through. It was clear that she had been listening. It was obvious she knew everything. I remember her long eyes were watery and red-rimmed. One thin hand held a cigarette, the other fiddled with the clasp of her handbag: open, shut, open, shut.

"Ready?" she asked Constantin. "It's almost time."

She lit her cigarette.

"You know, I knew you were special, from the moment I first set eyes on you," she said, as she picked a strand of tobacco from her mouth. "Because I once knew a man like you. I was a child, terminally ill, everyone had given up on me."

"Juliet," I intervened. "Could you give us five minutes?"

"He gave me hope," she said with suppressed force, as if the words had just slipped out before she could stop them. "He had faith."

Clara took the stage. She was wearing a red dress and dark red lipstick. Her face was expressionless as a silent movie star. Milo held three silver hoops. He lit them one by one and threw them to her.

"Nobody knows," I whispered. "Not for sure."

"I know," he replied.

On the stage, the blue of the flames and the red of the dress circled each other faster and faster until they became purple. Clara jumped like a cat and span like a top. She drew fiery ribbons in the air and danced through them. But the Pop Star was restless. He was sure he had seen acts like Clara's before. He sighed, he crossed his legs. On stage Clara was aware of it. She moved more quickly, she whirled and twirled and leapt higher. Her body became liquid, it poured itself from one movement into the next. She danced as if her life would be over if she did not give her all. She danced to be close to the curtains made for Louis IVX; she danced to show that she was precious too, she danced for everything she knew she deserved. It was devastating.

The Pop Star did not notice. He yawned. He stood up and wandered over to the buffet that nobody would eat. He ate a strawberry. Behind him Clara snapped. She dropped a burning hoop. She tried to retrieve it but could not. She landed awkwardly on one foot and twisted her ankle. The other two hoops dropped out of the air and rolled away. The performance juddered to a halt.

Constantin saw it all but was not watching. He was inches away from me but I could feel him slipping away. I was about to lose him again for certain.

"There must be something, something I can do." But I didn't mean it. Not really.

Constantin didn't look at me. He took a deep breath and then he nodded.

In the ballroom one pair of hands clapped, which made it even worse. Clara hobbled from the stage; the angles of her body hardened and set, the nails on her hands as sharp as rakes.

"Thank you," said the Pop Star. "That was very pretty."

"I'll call you," said Juliet.

Constantin led me through the darkened house. We padded along yard after yard of soft wool carpet. His hand was cold and damp. Outside I caught a glimpse of red tail lights through mottled glass. Milo and Clara were leaving. I suddenly wished they weren't. I realized that I was alone, more alone than I had ever been.

"Where are we going?" I asked.

But I knew. The former laundry.

It had been some time since I had been there and the room was almost unrecognisable. There were so many shelves and bottles that the walls seemed to curve inwards, like a cave. The wood-burning boiler was stoked high, making the room hot and humid. Hanging above it from three metal chains was a crucible. It glowed a dull green. As soon as we entered, Constantin stripped off the tuxedo. He pulled on a pair of old trousers and just for an instant I recognized the man he had been on the island, the man who had saved me. But when he reached for a bottle from the top shelf, I saw that he had stopped addressing me directly.

"You knew Milo?" he said. "How much else is there about you that I don't know."

"Does that matter? I've never loved anyone like I loved you," I said, and I meant it. "Please stop."

But how well do we ever know anyone? Probably not as well as we think. But there was no use in reasoning with him. I knew then that I was already a stranger to him, already an obstacle to his singular goal. The liquid he poured was clear and colourless. There would be no side effects, only a little pain and I would be fully recovered by the morning.

"I cannot have a child," he repeated. "Drink if what you say is true."

He held out the potion to me in a small crystal whisky glass. His hand shook very slightly as he waited for me to take it. I was suddenly filled with horror, with loathing, with grief. Was this really what he wanted? Was this the culmination of everything that had happened to us?

"Constantin?" I said, searching his face for an answer.

"Well?" he said, and he looked at me at last.

It was a challenge. It was the final push. And I was toppled. I said the first thing that came into my head.

"It's not yours."

His mouth opened and I saw him repeat the three words to himself, trying to make sense of them. And then it closed. He understood. In his eyes I read first relief, and then betrayal. He nodded. There was nothing left to say. Not anymore.

Behind him a white stone floated in the crucible like a fallen moon.

The cake was three tiers high and decorated with sugar daisies. The Pop Star cut the smallest cake into a dozen pieces, which nobody would eat. Juliet handed me a cheque, which I doubted I would ever cash.

Constantin took the stage at half past midnight. At the last moment he had decided to wear his bear coat. The rain had stopped and the world outside was silent. He started with a repeat of the show he had performed at Glasgow Green. But this time there was no fumbling with powders or accidental spillages. He handled bottles and vials, lighted tapers and ice with ease. His hand was steady and his touch was deft and confident. In fact his performance was almost a slow complicated dance, the way he reached and poured and stepped and hopped.

The Pop Star was mesmerized. He laughed, he sighed, he clapped spontaneously. Constantin, however, was unaware of the effect he was having on his audience of one. His fingers seemed to quiver; each breath was inhaled through the flare of his nostrils. His whole body was cocked.

I watched him from the back of the ballroom. I was full of rage, boiling with fury, brimming with spite. At that point I hated him more than I had ever hated anyone. Right then and there I wanted him to die. I really did.

A small Bunsen burner had been placed beneath the crucible that held the white stone. Constantin lit it with one strike of a long black match.

"And now," he said. "I will demonstrate the last stage of six. I will create the red rose, the Azoth, the elixir of life—the Philosopher's Stone."

He paused. The ballroom was completely silent, silent apart from the grate of a jet plane in the night sky and the distant siren of an ambulance.

At Constantin's side was a small glass of water. He picked it up and poured it into the crucible in one steady stream. And then at his instruction, we stood back. The liquid hissed, bubbled and died down. I braced myself for an explosion, an outpouring of poisonous gases or at least a spark of light but nothing happened. The white stone was still clearly visible. Constantin swallowed twice and turned up the flame.

"We have to wait," Constantin said "for it to reach the right temperature."

We waited. Five minutes passed. And then ten. The Pop Star leaned back in his chair. His shoulders clenched and he started to tap his foot. He was steeling himself for another disappointment. Juliet rubbed her temple with one long-fingered hand. She didn't dare hum. Suddenly the silence was broken by the scrape of a chair.

"That's it," the Pop Star said. "Game's over. Please get your stuff together and get out. You must think me an idiot. Juliet, you're fired."

And then the white stone cracked and spat, making the Pop Star jump back. Steam rose up in a lilac cloud, momentarily obscuring Constantin. When his face reappeared, I barely recognized him. His eyes were screwed tight shut and he seemed to have aged. Then he opened his eyes.

"Look!" he said, "look!"

The crucible glowed red, the red of a hand cupping a light bulb.

The Pop Star finally looked. He was scared.

"You've done it, you've really done it?!"

Constantin stared at the crucible.

"The Philosopher's Stone," he said. "The Azoth, the elixir of life... a substance which can change any metal to gold and cure all ills."

I stared at Constantin. Was this the face of a man who was about to die? His whole life was written bold: the hope, the faith, the sacrifice.

"I told you," said Juliet, "I told you he was special... I've seen it before, you see..."

Her voice tailed off.

"Well," said the Pop Star. "Does it work?"

"Let's find out," said Constantin with a small smile.

He raised two fingers of one hand to his mouth and then very carefully he lowered them into the crucible.

The Pop Star gasped. Juliet turned away. The stone was red hot. Surely he would burn himself.

"It's cool," said Constantin. "Just the way it is supposed to be."

He pulled a fifty pence coin from his pocket and held it between his thumb and forefinger.

"Come and watch," he said. "This coin will be transformed. The Azoth can change any matter from impure to pure, from one state to another."

He placed the coin in the crucible and closed his eyes in

anticipation of the miracle that was about to happen. Juliet and the Pop Star moved closer while I moved back. I crouched behind some chairs. I covered my head. I braced myself for an explosion, I waited for the crack and boom of detonation. Seconds ticked by. Nothing happened. A TV set in the servants' quarters was switched on. Distant gunfire ricocheted up the stairs. Finally, I looked up. And I could tell instantly from Juliet's anxious face that the coin in crucible was still just a tarnished fifty pence piece.

The truth hit me quite suddenly. It was a rush of ice cold air, a moment of cool-headed clarity. The sixth stage would not kill Constantin the way I'd imagined. The Red Stone was not dangerous but inert. The disaster that had befallen the alchemists on Sleat Rock was most likely the result of angry destruction rather than a tragic accident. No, the only thing it would damage was the one that Constantin had chosen above all else; his belief.

And I was filled with pity for him.

With one hand, I had opened a mirrored door. With another, I had turned on the mirrored ball. Nobody saw me climb the stage. Nobody saw me step between the crucible and the alchemist. But before I did what I had set out to do, I turned towards my lover, your father, and I leaned upwards until my mouth was close to his. I could not help myself. In, out, in, out; we breathed the same air for what I knew would be the last time.

A breeze blew open a window in another room. The mirrored door was blown open an inch. My cover shifted for a couple of seconds and I shimmered like an apparition. Constantin opened his eyes and found me, right there in front of him.

"Helena?"

I snatched the cool red stone from the crucible and then stepped back into the beam of light. He tried to grab me but I was too quick.

"No," he shouted. "No…"

The last time I saw him, Constantin was lashing around wildly like a blind man, trying in vain to find me. Juliet and the Pop Star were huddled together behind the cake. They must have thought that Constantin had flipped. The empty crucible was blackening on the yellow flame.

It was easier to slip away from the Pop Star's mansion than it was to get in. The servants' entrance wasn't locked. I walked across fields and along swollen rivers all night and most of the next day until I came out a small town. In the distance I heard the tinkle and wheeze of a carousel and saw the coloured lights of a travelling circus pitched at the mouth of a small river.

The Great Barrissimo and his wife Elsie were not particularly surprised when I knocked on their caravan door.

"Running away with the circus, dear?" Elsie asked me over a mug of boiled tea. "Now then, what can you do?"

"Nothing," I replied.

"Well that's as good a place to start as any," Elsie said.

That night I lay on a bed in a caravan as the rain dripped rhythmically on to my pillow, and sobbed. This time, bonds had been broken that could never be fixed. The red stone in my pocket had turned the colour of dried mud. In the pitch black of a wet, moonless night, I threw the stone as hard as I could into the slow flowing river. It sunk beneath the surface with a small insignificant splash.

The next day, we hitched up and headed south. You were born five months later, in the middle of the night. I forget the town, so you'll have to check your birth certificate. In the space where the name of the father should have been written there is a blank. You may fill it in now if you wish. As I have already written, you were absolutely perfect. I believe that you were the miracle he tried so hard to make in his crucible, a miracle made of the sweat of stars and mercury, sulphur and salt.

Little Wing, I was never the type to flick to the back of the book before I had finished. I always believed that endings should stay where they belong, in the last pages. Twice in my life I have been privy to information that I should not have been. Magnus' words were the first. The second was just before you were born. I won't go into graphic detail but when the midwife was listening to your heart she heard mine. My premature birth had left me with a heart with a hole blown clear through it. The fact that I had survived so many high wire stunts, the doctors told me, was nothing short of miraculous. One more tiny explosion, however, and it would stop beating for sure. Suddenly the ending of my story was approaching, ready or not. The only way to prolong my life would have been to spend the rest of it in bed and send you out for adoption. Otherwise, they ascertained, I would not last out the month. You see, I read too many books when I was a child. I just expected to grow old. When I found out that this was not to be, I worked out that my story, however brief, made a certain sense. Bed rest and torpor were never an option. And so I gathered you up and stayed with the Great Barrissimo's circus. I could give you two things. One you have almost finished. The other is endless. Oh, and just in case you were wondering, I'm afraid the Pop Star's cheque bounced.

It is almost light outside. And still you sleep. You have grown faster than a miracle, quicker than corn. I feel so close to you that I cannot believe that soon it shall be time to let you go. We shall meet again, my dear. I know it is so. I know it.

I must say goodbye to you, the little girl who sleeps in the crook of my arm, forcing me to type with one hand. My tale, I know, is far-fetched and a mite unbelievable. None, I hasten to add, none of it is the product of invention, all of it happened to me, verbatim. Anyway, this is my legacy. This and my story. What have I learned? Always leap rather than risking the chance, however slight, of disappearing.

I come out of my box. Into another box, my flat. Now empty. No furniture. No books, No TV. Just my rings, hanging-swaying, one in one direction and the other, in the other. As if someone's just gone. I felt her close for so long and now when I try and sense her, I can't anymore.

Another day has opened its lids. Light spills in. My body is dead from all that squash-hiding but when I shake-loosen it, I know I don't want to die anymore.

And then I see the rope, the long grey metal rope which links one block with the other, links them so they both fall as one and not in opposite directions which might squash people accidentally. That's what all the noisebangcrashing was.

I swing towards the balcony. Up here I have lost the knack of time but down there it's still early. I can see the motorway gliding with the blue bottle buzz of traffic, the shopping centre with its scattering of cars, the gasometer, its big fat tummy still full up, and there, as always, the oily slide of the river.

The men in yellow hats are up early too. Building a fence to keep back the spectators. They have boarded up the doors, knocked down the lower stairs in case of opportunistic suicides. The people who come to watch as boom, sigh, crash, my house falls down, already fill up the play park and the DIY store car park.

I was a circus child. I could swing before I could walk, cartwheel before I could count. What happened to me? I see it now. My story ended. I grew too big. That was why my legs stopped working.

I look down at my legs now, my long thin legs soft with blond down and with knees all covered in scars and I let them stretch and flex. They are perfect, after all.

I stand up. I am taller than a house, taller than a cloud. I am not little anymore. Slow, slowly I reach forward, over the balcony and very gently touch the rope. With one long shudder, one snakeish slither, the rope turns from grey to gold before my eyes. And then, only then, do I look up. Across. And there you are. Of course, of course.

Before I change my mind, before I bottle out and lose my stupid nerve, I climb over the balcony until my legs are weightless swinging in the cold morning air. The sun has finally come up and dazzles me. Below, the sheer drop of thirty-five balconies down to the ground. It's a long way to fall.

The golden rope is cold and slightly slippery beneath my feet.

My arms are flung right out and I imagine they have grown feathers. I don't look down. I never do. My name is Wing. Instead I look at you, you with your thick hair, turned silver, you with your eyes which slant up, just a little, at the corners, at you, Constantin, the bear man.

"That was a very stupid thing to do," you say when I reach your balcony.

"It was the only way," I say.

Inside your flat is as bare as mine, but everything is mirror opposite, the doors in the other wall, the light falling backwards.

We look at each other and I have this strangest sensation that I have been looking at your face for the whole of my life. And I have, because you look like me. And then I notice a letter on the table, typed on the same thin white paper as my mother's manuscript.

"I searched you know," you say, "I searched and searched until I realized that it was not the stone she had stolen that I was looking for anymore, but her."

Your eyes speak of sadness and joy, hot and cold, faith and doubt.

I look away. I suddenly don't know what to say. On the floor is an old notebook. I pick it up. Inside are diagrams and lists written in Russian. They look like recipes. The ink at the start is faded but towards the back the ink is black and new. You take it from my hands.

"I gave it up but I was always drawn back," you say. "There are some things you can't live without. Even things that you've broken with your own two hands. "

I suddenly feel angry. Furious in fact. My own father, a man who would forsake his own child.

"If you knew about me," I say. "Why didn't you say something?"

You look at me and your mouth starts to curl, the way my mother said it did.

"What, like how do you do?"

I don't laugh. It isn't funny.

"Your mother's lawyer spent many months tracking me down," you say. "I only just found out... forgive me."

Outside the sirens start to wail. A chill wind comes through the window. You pull a coat around you, a coat made of bear. The countdown begins, ten... nine.

"It feels like the end of something," you say.

"Or the beginning," I reply.

When I step on the rope again there is a great cuffuful down below. It is lucky that the wind is so still because they rush around with their yellow hats for ages before, as I guessed they would, the fire brigade stretch out their white sheet thing and shout, "'Jump! Jump!'"

And so I close my eyes and imagine I am back up on the platform again, back up high in the pinch of the tent where the cobwebs are heavy with tiny jewels of moisture, the air is filled with drifts of dust like fine, fine snow and the wire sings. I breathe in quick and feel the cold air fill me up inside with shivers and blue glow. And then I jump.

But it's not over yet. Oh no. I land in clouds of white and the hands of strong young men. Then I climb down and am smothered in tears and hugs by Julie who has somehow sneaked past the security guards and the dogs. In clogs, too.

"Wait!" I tell the fire brigade as they start to start to fold up the sheet. "I wasn't alone."

Julie thinks I have gone insane, that I can walk again but I am now mad instead.

"There's nobody up there," she says, her glasses misting up.

"Look where I came from before I jumped," I say. "Not my block but the other."

And then there's a lot of shouting and cross words and conversations into walkie-talkies as I insist that you, my father, are still on the top floor, and Julie, who always knows best, contradicts me.

With perfect timing, a bear, or rather a man in a bear coat

appears and shakily shakily walks along the golden rope for a few yards. Not bad for someone who's clearly never done it before. Everybody stops talking and looks up at you so tiny and small up there, a tense pencil dash against the wide square of sky.

You pause. You're not going to do it. You will fall the wrong way or dash your head against multiple balconies. It has all been in vain. Me. You. My mother's story.

"Noooo!" I shout, without being able to help it, my voice carried up up like a siren only much much sadder.

But then, you stand up straight and take off the coat and toss it. It falls floor after floor, turning and billowing and landing in a dead, crumpled heap. And then you look down, you breathe in deep. And you leap.

Acknowledgements

Thanks to *The* Toby Press, my editor Aloma Halter, Giles Gordon, Kathryn Heyman and Miranda France.

About the author

Beatrice Colin

Beatrice Colin was born in London and grew up in Scotland. A journalist for several newspapers, she has written on a wide range of subjects, including Paris fashion, blood feuds in Albania, contemporary art, and motherhood.

Her short stories have appeared in various publications in Britain and America, including *The London Magazine* and *Ontario Review.*

She writes screenplays, radio adaptatons and plays, several of which have been broadcast by BBC radio. Her debut novel, *Nude Untitled,* was short-listed for the Saltire First Book Award and has won her admirers in the UK and USA.

She currently lives and works in Brooklyn with her husband and two small children.

*The fonts used in this book are from the
Garamond and Rosewood families*

Other works by Beatrice Colin are published by The Toby Press

Nude Untitled